Teaching Ms. Riggs

Stephanie Beck

LYRICAL PRESS
Kensington Publishing Corp.
www.kensingtonbooks.com

First Electronic Edition: September 2011
eISBN-13: 978-1-61650-315-4
eISBN-10: 1-61650-315-7

First Print Edition: Setpember 2011
ISBN-13: 978-1-61650-841-8
ISBN-10: 1-61650-841-8

Printed in the United States of America

It'll take a special man to teach her to live again.

Benfri (Ben) Riggs has come home to Flatthead Falls, Missouri to heal. After her husband's murder, secrets behind the peaceful, successful life she thought they'd shared emerge to leave her deep in debt, infertile, and afraid for her life. Teaching chemistry in her old hometown is her shout of independence, even though she wants to crawl under her bed in fear when the terrorizing phone calls begin.

Mark Dougstat works the land, makes things grow, and isn't ashamed of the occasional mess his shoes cause. Busy making his farm pay enough to support his niece and nephew, he hasn't found the time or inclination to make the time, to find a good woman. Ben Riggs's humor and compassion change that fast.

But they're going to have a battle on their hands. Ben's stalker won't quit. What is between Ben and Mark grows and they push forward in their relationship, learning more secrets along the way. Before they can settle into life together, the stalker will strike again. Blood will be shed and lives changed forever in the blink of an eye. Can they trust each other enough to get them through?

Books by Stephanie Beck

Teaching Ms. Riggs
Unraveling Midnight

Published by Kensington Publishing Corporation

For my mother.

Chapter 1

Another box. What the hell was she going to do with another wad of cardboard? She had no idea, and she refused to walk to the dumpster after dark even if she was back in her hometown. The only place with room was the tiny space between the refrigerator and wall, so she crammed it in with the others.

Benfri Riggs turned and surveyed her apartment. It was small, sparse and ugly. The walls were the same color yellow she'd promised herself never to be surrounded by after her two years in dorms. The sofa sagged, and the TV needed a converter box. The super had promised to bring her a spare box, and in the meantime, her tiny MP3 player provided the only source of background noise.

Classical music filled the silence. That's all she needed, because she wasn't really paying attention to it anyway. She ambled across her kitchen, three whole steps, and grabbed a box of cereal from above the refrigerator. The afternoon spent unpacking had been a blissful time of non-thought.

Unfortunately, her stomach growled and exhaustion loomed, so it was time to sit down and eventually go to bed. She poured milk into her bowl after the cereal. The cheap brand didn't taste the greatest, but it would suffice until she got her first paycheck.

She tried not to wince at the first bite, reminding herself she wasn't some spoiled wife anymore. How she'd ended up one, she still didn't quite understand. She'd been raised in Flathead Falls, Missouri, with a box of the same store-brand corn flakes on the breakfast table every morning.

Maybe if her aunt had splurged on the frosted ones once in a while, Ben wouldn't have been so drawn to Don and his slick ways. The thought made her grin, but it was much too easy to blame her fastidious, spendthrift aunt for the turn Ben's life had taken. She took another bite and did wince.

She missed coffee from anywhere but her own cheap coffee pot. Giving up everything had been for the best, but she still wished for the things she couldn't have anymore. She looked over her shoulder at the stack of bank papers she'd lugged from Chicago. Because of her husband's past criminal activities, she hadn't been granted the bankruptcy she needed after his death.

Instead, she'd been saddled with an unbelievable loan with interest that made her stomach turn. She tossed her spoon aside and rested her forehead on the heel of her hand.

This was why she couldn't stop moving. When she did the weight of her heavy world settled between her shoulder blades and made the moments unbearable. Not only had she lost her husband and been overwhelmed with debt, she'd had to learn from strangers just who the man she'd loved really was. A criminal, identity thief, adulterer and, the worst offense in her mind, a drug dealer who preyed on children.

She shook off her pity party, or at least told herself she had to before she drove herself crazy. Ben took her bowl and spoon to the sink and slowly washed them, killing time to keep the ugly thoughts away, but they invaded full force.

The police officer who had informed her all about Don had worn a smirk the entire time as he detailed Don's dealings and personal liaisons. Instead of treating her like the victim she was, the detective had taken great pleasure in presenting her with pictures of Don with other women.

That file was under the one from the bank. She should have burned it, but she couldn't. It was a good reminder of what being stupid could bring. Love wasn't the negative, it was the things she'd done for love that made her regret ever meeting Don.

She'd given him everything and trusted him when he asked her to. It had never occurred to her to question him.

Ben turned off the light in the kitchen so only the living room lamp remained. Classic rock now filled the room.

There was absolutely no sense in thinking about the past. She scolded herself as she checked the multitude of locks on the door. The only thing the past had that she had to worry about was a single woman who may or may not have been the one to kill Don. But even she wasn't going to take over Ben's mind.

Determined to make the best of the night, Ben grabbed her briefcase and looked through the papers. As she organized class lists and introduction letters, she reminded herself that she needed to look toward the future.

One good thing had come from her time with Don--her teaching license. Back in her hometown she had found a way to start paying her crippling debt by doing what she'd been trained for: teaching chemistry. She smiled as she started making notes, the ugliness behind her as she focused. Nothing would hold her back this time.

Chapter 2

"Let's see, I need Thomas LeDoux at my desk after class. Who's Thomas, again?"

Ben hated asking for their names but she was one person in a sea of smelly fifteen and sixteen year olds, mostly boys. Over seventy percent of the sophomore class was male, and she couldn't even begin to think of a reason why that would be the case.

To make things harder on her exhausted mind, most of them had basic, Midwest names. There were four 'Johns' in her first hour homeroom, along with several 'Marks' and 'Lukes'. She checked her paper and realized the Thomas she'd just called was one of five she'd seen so far. It was going to be a long day.

A lanky, dark-haired boy raised his hand from the last row of tables. Guilt trickled in because she should have remembered his name and face, but until she'd corrected his paper, nothing about him had stood out. She'd been skeptical when he'd breezed through the test, handing it in only halfway through the period. After she'd looked it over, she'd changed her tune. Contrary to his nondescript exterior, the boy was a genius according to the results.

She smiled as he ambled his way to her desk, his lanky frame making it more work than necessary. The bell rang before he made it to her. The same one that had freed her from her classrooms so many years ago when she'd walked Flathead Falls' High School halls.

"All right, guys, don't run. Remember to get all those papers signed tonight, boys and Megan and Shelly." Ben nodded and smiled to the only two girls in class as they passed out the door behind the boys.

"Did I do something wrong, Ms. Riggs?"

Ben turned to the young man before her. His voice had cracked horribly, and his cheeks burned red in embarrassment. She remembered those days when her body had often betrayed her.

"Absolutely not, Thomas. I just need to talk with you for a minute. I'll write you a pass for your next class."

"No problem, I just have lunch." The young man's voice evened out a bit and was a deep baritone. It was a very nice sound, and he'd probably have the girls lining up as soon as he grew into his nose and lanky bird legs.

After giving Thomas's test one last look, she handed it to him. He took it with confusion on his face.

"Was there something wrong?" he asked, looking it over with sharp eyes. "I put my name on it, right?"

"Yes, you remembered your name. Actually, the reason I wanted to talk with you is because there is nothing wrong with your test. At all. Is it something you've had a history with?" Fatigue made Ben reach for her stool. After she straddled it, she motioned for Thomas to take the seat across her desk.

He sat, his long frame slouching, though she saw he attempted to sit straight on the stool with no back.

"Uh, yeah, I guess I've done some of it before." He fidgeted with the ripped edge of his book binding.

She thought he might be a little nervous and amped up her smile. Instilling fear in her students was something she hoped to wait a few more weeks to do.

"My parents are pharmaceutical scientists. I spent the summer in France with them, mostly with my father in his lab."

Ben could tell he hadn't thought much of the experience even if he'd learned from it. The scowl on his face wasn't a rebellious one. Thomas just looked genuinely unhappy at the memory. Her first instinct was to reach across the desk and pat his shoulder or offer some kind of comfort, but she refrained because it wasn't quite appropriate.

"What did you think of the test?" she asked, hoping to get him on a different topic.

"Ah, it was pretty easy, I guess. I'd seen all the stuff before, but I won't act out or anything in class, if you're worried. I'm sure there's lots of stuff I can learn from you."

Ben smiled at his quick cover. "I am pretty smart." She bit her tongue to keep from laughing when he blushed a little at his unintentional insult. "But here's the thing that concerns me, Thomas. This test was set up especially to be a full year sampling for sophomores to give me an idea of what everyone retained from previous years. Most people did really well on what they'd already learned, but there is a ton of new stuff on here and you blew through it like it was a colors quiz. You've got an advanced understanding of what I'm teaching basics for in this class. If it were just you and me, I could keep you busy, but that's not the case. I think you would do much better in Mr. Kai's class."

"Senior high chemistry?" he asked, his skepticism clear.

"Yes. I'll talk to the guidance counselor and Mr. Kai for approval, but thought I'd ask for your thoughts first."

He scratched his arm nervously before he replied, "I should probably talk to my uncle about it. Would it be a lot more homework? I don't want to get spread too thin with all my new classes and football."

"Maybe some, but not an unreasonable amount. I'd be happy to set up a meeting with your uncle, you, Mr. Kai and myself to answer any questions you and your uncle might have," she promised with a reassuring smile. His foresight was a pleasant surprise.

"Okay, yeah. Uncle Mark's number is on the card thing you handed out. Practice doesn't start until four o'clock today, so if you can make something work between three-thirty and four it would be better for me."

He pushed up from the stool onto his huge feet, reminding Ben of a young horse, still figuring out how to use all his limbs. She wondered how much he'd grown in the past summer to give him such difficulties. Her own growth spurts hadn't put her past five and a half feet, so she couldn't imagine the adjusting the poor kid was doing.

"I'll call your uncle on my lunch break, how's that sound?"

"Yeah, should work. Thanks, Ms. Riggs. Hey, is your name really Ben?"

"Actually, it's Benfri, which was my mother's maiden name."

"That's cool."

"I think so." She waved him out as students for her next class trickled in. "You'd better head to lunch. Stop in before practice. Hopefully we'll get this all ready for you."

* * * *

Must. Buy. Air freshener. Ben held her breath and smiled as her latest class filed out. Teenage boys smelled rough in the best scenario but the last group had come straight from gym class. She made a note to call the gym teacher and beg for deodorant reminders to be sent home.

Before she could see to the future preservation of her abused olfactory system, she had to open a window and call Thomas's uncle. With a fresh breeze permeating the room, she sighed in relief. The day was going well, but the break was incredibly welcomed.

To-do list in mind, she pulled Thomas's card from her box of contacts and, sure enough, no mom or dad was listed. He'd mentioned spending the summer with his parents in their lab, but there was no notation of either of them.

She was sure she would hear the story of Thomas's family before too long. As she'd been on the gossips' lips before, she knew the strength of the pipeline in small communities. Since the schools and churches were information central, she knew she wouldn't have long to wait for all the latest on everyone else's business.

She dialed the number and waited, her mind wandering to dinner as her stomach growled. The food was still as bad as it had ever been in the cafeteria, so she'd have to start bringing something from home. Cereal for three meals a day sounded horrible. Doable, but detestable.

"What?"

The harsh greeting jerked Ben out of her nutritional thoughts.

"Ah, Mr. Dougstat?"

"Yeah?"

"Hello, I'm Ben Riggs from Flathead Falls Schools. I'm Thomas's pre-chem teacher. There is something I would like to talk about with you and Thomas if you have time?"

"Yeah, what's that?" he demanded and cursed. "Damn. Can I call you back? I'm getting my butt kicked by a cow who doesn't want her shots right now. As long as Thomas and Kira are okay--"

"They are, absolutely." Understanding dawned and if he'd been fighting with a cow, she had to admit he was actually being pretty polite. "If you could come in at three-thirty today we could talk about it."

"Fine, Riggs, chem, three-thirty."

"Yep, good luck with the cow." Ben smiled when she put the phone back in the cradle.

It had been much too long since she'd even thought about cows. Her dad had raised dairy cattle and she'd always helped, but after he died, she'd never stepped foot back on a farm. Another bittersweet memory, she thought, with a long sigh.

Ben's last class of the day had just filed out when Mr. Kai arrived with Thomas at his heels already talking chemistry. To her relief she understood most of what they said and ended up laughing with them over lame science jokes. She was about to tell one of her own when something assaulted her nose.

Cow poop. It wasn't a new smell, not in rural Missouri, but so far it was one smell, thanks to clean shoes, she hadn't experienced in her classroom.

Ben watched the entry, not knowing what she expected in Thomas's uncle, but the tall man wearing a Flathead Falls ball cap with blond curls around the edge wasn't it.

He was fit and the source of the smell that clung to him wasn't obvious since his jeans looked old but fresh and his shoes were bright white. After cuffing his nephew on the shoulder in greeting, he looked over at Ben. She stopped thinking a moment when he smiled.

"Hello." He held out his hand. "I'm Mark Dougstat. Are you Ms. Riggs?"

Remembering she was a professional, Ben shook herself and extended her hand as well. "Yes, I am. Thanks for making it in on such short notice."

"No problem. So, what's this all about?"

Ben explained about Thomas's test and then let Mr. Kai take over. She listened as the older teacher went over his syllabus and how his class worked. Thomas and his uncle listened intently, Mark nodding several times and asking questions along the way.

Smart questions, she thought. He was obviously close to his nephew to worry about his workload. She found herself smiling for no reason except for the pleasure she felt in listening to his voice and ordered herself to stop. She hadn't come home to fall head over heels for the first man who smiled at her. No matter how nice of a smile he had.

"Can you handle it?" Mark asked as Thomas looked over the text and a few sample tests.

"Yep." The youth was already engrossed in a page full of equations and barely looked up. "Some of these are pretty hard."

Mr. Kai laughed. "Good. I'd like to think there could be some challenge for you. Ms. Riggs has already offered to set up some enrichment opportunities to really challenge you in your downtime in my class."

"Your uncle might have to help you with some of them," Ben added, and Mark snorted a little. "Not so great with chemistry?"

"Not even slightly," he replied and sent her a little wink. Ben fought a blush, but didn't think she succeeded as he continued, "But I do make a hell of an after-school snack. I also stock the drawer with freshly sharpened pencils."

"His marshmallow crispy squares are awesome." Thomas's loyal pledge was ruined when he laughed and elbowed his uncle. "Especially when he wraps them in the little blue foil with the elves on it."

"Big mouth," Mark muttered, but he smiled too. "Do I have to sign anything to make the switch?"

Ben was so charmed by the way the two males acted with each other she didn't realize at first the question was for her.

"Ms. Riggs?" Mr. Kai asked, and she started. This time she didn't even attempt to stop her blush.

"Ah, thing to sign...nope. We just wanted to okay it with you since the guidance counselor already said it was fine. Oh, Thomas, doesn't football start soon?"

"Yeah, I gotta go." He stood, already in his pads and cleats. Ben thought he looked a little like a kid in adult clothes. One day he would grow into himself and he'd be a bruiser. "See ya at home, Uncle Mark."

"Bye, buddy. Play hard. I'll get your books and finish up here. Need anything from the store?"

"Gatorade," Thomas called over his shoulder as he hustled out of the room. "And fruit snacks and peanut butter."

Ben smiled at his response. Throughout the day food had been the main topic of conversation for most of the young men. If they weren't talking about the granola bar in their locker, then they were trying to sweet talk the girls out of the fruit snacks they had in theirs.

Ben was still smiling when Mr. Kai took off to pick up his daughter. Alone with Mark, she turned again and tried to find some similarities between lanky Thomas and this hunk of man in front of her.

Mark was thickly muscled across the shoulders. He'd taken off his hat, and his hair was thick and mostly blond. He had to be in or near his forties by the deep lines around his eyes, but those could have been from the climate too. Farmers lived hard. Ben had a feeling though, by the pattern of the lines, that Mark also laughed hard. She wondered if Thomas would be like him eventually. Young men changed so much in only a few short years.

Mark flipped through the chemistry book, not really reading, Ben thought. He might have been looking at the pictures but nothing in depth. He looked up at her with questions in his gray-blue eyes.

He closed the book and stacked it with the other papers. "So? Anything else I should know?"

"Nope. That's about everything I can think of, but don't hesitate to call if Thomas is having troubles. I don't anticipate problems, but if they pop up I'm happy to help with tutoring."

"That's nice, thanks." Mark shuffled the books and papers, a classic delay tactic. Ben bit back a smile as she watched him shift them from back to front again as he made no attempt to leave the room. "I'll fill out this stuff tonight and send it with Thomas tomorrow."

"Oh, just a second." If she didn't get the numbers she'd be in trouble, so she reached for the books. Their hands collided for the second time. The handshake had been nice, but the casual, innocent touch was much more and she fought herself from blushing like one of her students. "I, um, need to write down the numbers."

He grinned and slid the book across the table, the back of his hand brushing against hers again, and she shivered.

"No problem, Ms. Riggs. I sure wouldn't want to cause any clerical problems."

She quickly opened the book and tried to be professional and efficient as she added Thomas's name to the inside cover and into her ledger. Mark's gaze settled on her, and once again she scolded herself for even thinking about flirting or being flattered. She had no business smiling at nice men with the trouble following her.

"Okay, there you go." Taking special pains not to touch him, she slid the book back. "The other is a workbook he needs to keep close track of because it has a lot of his homework for the year. Oh, and Thomas mentioned his parents are in France. Should I add them to my contact lists or put their address down for sending report cards to or anything?"

Mark shook his head, the sparkle of his smile slightly diminishing. "I take care of all of his school stuff, so don't worry about his parents. I'll make sure he knows about the workbook, but I know he'll take good care of it."

"I'm sure he's very responsible," Ben said, wondering if the flirting had been killed by the subject of Thomas's parents, which was obviously uglier than she'd thought.

"Well, I wouldn't go that far, but I do have him changing his socks every day now." His sense of humor was back and with it came the playful feelings that had been bubbling in her since his arrival.

When Mark's smile deepened again, she at least had the boost of knowing she wasn't alone in the unexpected attraction. She was ready to put a stop on her bubbles and be completely professional when he winked. It had the same effect as earlier and heat crawled up her neck. She hadn't been winked at in years, let alone twice in one sitting.

"Um..." What did one say when they were winked at?

"Is there anything else I need to do or have Thomas do? Any first day homework? Maybe we should have him read the first chapter or ten?"

"No homework yet." She smiled at his impish grin and was thankful for the reprieve from having to respond to the wink. His nature was infectious, and it crossed her mind that he probably winked at all the girls and had a line waiting for him somewhere. That helped her focus on the situation again. "I'm sure he'll have plenty before long."

"First two chapters it is," he replied, tucking the books under his arm. "Don't worry, Ms. Riggs, the extra work will be good for the boy."

She laughed out loud and might have let herself forget about the probable gaggle of women falling in his charming wake if a student hadn't come in with a big basket.

"Hey, Susan. Can I help you?"

The girl trudged over and unloaded her burden. She stepped away and let out a theatric sigh. Ben wasn't sure she'd ever get used to such drama.

"Ms. Riggs, I'm so glad you're still here. My mom had this in her room and forgot to bring it down. I was supposed to set it on your desk, but here ya go. All the new teachers get one, kind of a welcome basket. So welcome."

"Thank you. This is so nice. Did your mother put it together?"

"No way. The school board members bring stuff to add, I just deliver. Gotta go, Mom's waiting." The girl took off with energy Ben envied after a long day.

She pulled the card from the ribbon on the top and skimmed over it, stopping short when she came to a typed name. "Hey, you're on here. Mark Dougstat."

"Yeah, I help with sports stuff." His embarrassed tone was a far cry from the teasing he'd been doing only moments earlier. The change was intriguing, but she focused on the card.

"Oh yeah? I guess that makes sense since Thomas is in sports. I love this birdhouse, who makes them?"

"Ah, I do. It's my hobby." His cheeks tinged pink in the most adorable way she'd ever seen. "My niece paints them for me."

"Well, it's all just wonderful. It's so good to be home."

"That's right, you're from here, aren't you?" he asked, making no move to leave. "Daniel and Sarah Riggs's daughter, right?"

"Yeah, and the Miss Benfri who worked at the library for decades is my aunt. I left for college in Chicago when I was seventeen, and now I'm back." She stayed vague with details because she wasn't ready to give anything more specific to him or anyone else in town. There were wounds still too new to discuss, and she wanted a fresh start. "It's good to be back. I didn't realize how much I'd missed it."

"Yeah, it grows on ya," Mark agreed and stood. Ben knew she should be relieved they were finally parting ways, but part of her wanted him to stay. "Well, I suppose I'd better hit the grocery store before Thomas gets home and finds the refrigerator without Gatorade or fruit snacks."

"It was nice meeting you, Mark." She offered her hand again. The simple handshake indulged a tiny bit of her need for contact, at least it was appropriate. "Oh, and I believe Thomas mentioned peanut butter. You wouldn't want to forget that."

"Heaven forbid. You have a good night, Ms. Riggs." He shook as professionally as before, but she didn't miss the added squeeze at the end and wondered if he'd had as much fun as she did in their simple, playful exchange. It was too bad nice men who were also ruggedly handsome and funny weren't in her sphere anymore. The wonderfully crooked smile was not for and could never be hers.

"It's Ben, actually. I only have my students call me Ms. Riggs."

"Ben, Benfri right?"

She nodded and waited for the questions that nearly always followed about her name.

"Ben it is." Mark smiled. "Welcome home."

Chapter 3

After looking through the basket and finding a fifty dollar gift certificate from the chamber of commerce, Ben headed directly to the grocery store. She'd been prepared to live on cereal until her first paycheck, but with the discovery came the promise of protein, or at least cheap hotdogs.

She grabbed a cart and smiled as she faced the familiar store. Everything was exactly where it had been the last time she'd walked the aisles nearly a decade earlier with her aunt. With a step much lighter than when she'd started her day, she headed down the first aisle.

The packages were updated for the most part, but there was a bit of a time warp as she passed the more southern grits and in a real flashback to her childhood, lard. She hadn't had lard fried chicken in years, and her butt thanked her for that. The grits though, they might be something she'd revisit soon.

Trying to be practical, she bought better cereal, string cheese, milk, canned fruit, canned soups and bread because it was all easy and so far she didn't have anything more than a small soup pan to cook in. With Thomas's request staying in her mind and sounding fantastic she grabbed peanut butter and looked longingly at the jelly, but her budget didn't allow it and her thighs didn't need it.

She loosened up her thigh and budget rules when she got to the freezer aisle. She allowed an indulgence because she was human and dealt with teenagers all day. A carton of double chocolate chip called her name, and she knew that at the end of the day it would be cold, sweet and chocolaty delicious. Ice cream was a perfectly respectable crutch for her at times. Even her Aunt Willy, the sourest woman Ben knew, never begrudged a little treat on occasion.

She looked at the carton in her hand and frowned when she noticed the torn plastic around the edges. The next one in the case was ripped too. There was no way she was going to buy freezer burned ice cream. Ben leaned down and reached for the third in line. There were other options, but she still went for the good stuff. She could always try vanilla, but really. Why bother?

* * * *

Mark turned into the freezer section. His mental list hadn't seemed that big when he'd left the house, but as he shopped he remembered how much food Thomas had gone through in the past three days. Since he was in town and at the store, he might as well re-stock the pantry.

The six week reprieve while the kids had been in France with their parents had been nice in a few ways. The grocery bill and sheer amount of time he'd spent at the store had reduced drastically. But he was making up for it now.

Thomas had grown six inches, all legs which were constantly empty, so there was never enough food in the house. Mark remembered those days, but still, the never-ending flow going into the kid astounded him.

Not to be outshined, Kira had decided to become a vegetarian. A nine-year-old anti-meat eater who lived on a working dairy farm where they raised a few beef cattle for cash on the side was not ideal.

Mark shook his head as he threw a bag of frozen cheese ravioli in the cart. He hoped the vegetarianism thing was a phase. There was nothing endearing about hearing every time he ate a steak that eating anything with a face made him a cannibal.

He remembered potpies and headed down the second freezer aisle. When he looked up from tossing the pies in his cart he caught sight of a generous backside filling out a khaki skirt. Ben Riggs. Despite the recent and much too brief introduction, he'd recognize her anywhere.

Part of him wished they'd known each other before she left Flathead Falls. She was quite a few years younger than him so they'd never hung out together. Watching her straighten and toss her hair back, he smiled. He would have liked having memories of Ben.

But he didn't mind the new memory he was making of her. Her thighs were the rounded, strong kind like the women who played catcher on softball teams. They looked muscular and tough but still soft to the touch. When she bent slightly forward he could have groaned at the pretty picture she made. Her thighs and hips led to a waist that was maybe a little chubby, but he'd never really paid enough attention to women to give an honest comparison.

He just knew he liked what he saw, a healthy, soft woman.

"Well, hello, Ben." Mark moved next to her cart to grab the largest tub of vanilla ice cream the store carried. "Sure is nice to see you again so soon."

"Oh, hi." Ben eyed his overflowing cart with a bemused smile. "I bet you have to do this often with a teenage boy at home."

"And don't forget his little sister, who can go pound for pound on most things during a growth spurt." Mark added a jug of chocolate syrup from the stand beside the freezer case. "And at the end of the day you'll be hard pressed to find a farm boy who doesn't like a bowl of ice cream."

"I bet. So you have both of the kids?"

"Yep. You haven't heard the whole story yet?" he asked, the market quiet in the pre-supper rush. She shook her head and the pretty corkscrew curls that had been locked in a clip slipped free. He wondered if she knew how distracting she was, but forged on to answer her question, "Their mom is my older sister. She's married to a French scientist. Kimmy is a scientist too, and they work on cancer drugs over in a French lab. She and her husband spend most of their time working, and they wanted the kids to be educated here. I was elected as guardian."

Ben paused in front of another case and turned to him. She had freckles. How could he have overlooked them when they met in the classroom? Must have been her eyes, Mark thought as her gaze connected with his again. Her kind of eyes could make a man forget his name.

"That's so great of you, Mark. They're lucky to have such a generous uncle. Do you help coach football? I was invited thirty-seven times today to go to the freshman and b-squad games on Thursday night and was wondering if you might know what time I should be there?"

"Six if you can. I don't help coach, but I try to make it to all of Thomas's games. Kira does too. They usually last an hour tops, so we get back in time for milking." The reminder made him look at his watch and bite back a curse. Now that he was getting another chance with Ben he wanted to make the most of it, but duty called. "Speaking of chores, I didn't realize how late it was getting. I better get home."

* * * *

"Yeah, same here. I should get going before my ice cream melts." Ben laughed and followed Mark with her sparsely filled cart.

She should have known better, but when she chose checkouts she went with the younger cashier. By the time the girl had rung up ten items, the old pro at the register Mark had gone to was finished. Ben paid and was thrilled to still have money left on the gift card even after splurging. She hefted the two bags and wished she'd driven her car.

With a sigh she headed for the door. Her apartment was only six blocks away. She could walk, and it would probably do her a lot of good. It wasn't like she was in a hurry anyway, so the walk would be fine.

"Ah damn, you aren't walking home, are you?" Mark appeared out of nowhere and plucked one of her bags from her arms. Her heart raced at the suddenness of his appearance, but she swallowed back the immediate fear. She had to remember she wasn't in Chicago anymore.

She cleared her throat and followed him after he put her bag in his cart. "Yes, I'm walking home. It's only a few blocks away. The Matterhast Apartments."

"Come on, I'll give you a ride. It's on my way, and your ice cream will melt for sure if you walk in this heat." He motioned her to a dirty, eighties-style rust bucket that most likely had been a truck at one time.

She pasted on a smile as she followed him. Being told what to do was one of her least favorite things lately. She counseled herself to be patient with the well-intentioned man. Watching the way Mark's hips moved as he walked went a long way in soothing her irritation.

"You don't have to, Mark. I appreciate the offer but--"

"How long were you in Chicago?" he broke in without turning back to face her.

"Ah, almost a decade."

"Then you were gone long enough to forget how we do things in small towns. Let me refresh your memory. When someone needs a ride and another person has a vehicle, we share a ride. If someone needs a hose and their neighbor isn't using theirs, it's lent so they don't have to drive thirty miles to Wal-Mart."

He tossed bags into the truck's bed as he spoke. Resigned, Ben stepped closer and helped him load his groceries into the bins in the back.

When he looked over and grinned, her annoyance slipped away without her permission. He winked again. "It'll come back to you, I'm sure."

She laughed and settled the last bag in the bin.

"Smartass," she muttered. "Okay, you might be right about me still being in the Chicago mindset. Thank you for the offer and for the ride. I appreciate it."

"There you go, sweetheart, it's coming back fast." He was teasing again like he had at the school, and she liked it. Browsing through the bags he looked up when he found her ice cream. "I've got a cooler back here. Want me to toss this in? The cab's gonna be hotter than hell and the AC is broken."

Tongue in cheek she gave an over-exaggerated sigh. "Of course it is. A broken AC and a hot running truck are prerequisites for any farm vehicle. Thanks for thinking of my ice cream."

She took her remaining bags and jumped into the truck while he corralled the cart. She coughed when the seat let loose a poof of gravel dust. Mark hopped in and the dust flew again.

"Sorry about that," he said with a light blush. "I would have brought the car if I thought anyone else would be riding with me. You can open your window if you want. The crank only sticks at first."

She turned the sticky manual lever as he started the truck. Belying the rust and age, the engine fired up with no hesitation. Thankfully, he had the truck moving in only a few seconds. The interior was so hot and stagnant that it took a block before fresh air circulated.

Ben said a small prayer of thankfulness for the tiny but ferocious window air conditioner that kept her apartment cool. She'd forgotten the power of a Missouri heat wave. Usually by September Chicago was cooling down, but Missouri had weeks left until even the nights became bearable.

The air conditioner at her apartment worked perfectly though, so she already pictured her night. The hum of the truck engine soothed her closer to the sleep her exhausted body craved. She could crank the air full blast, spread her paperwork on her bed and have a bowl of ice cream.

"I bet you're wrecked after a long day with all those kids." Mark's comment broke her out of her blessedly cool fantasy.

"Oh, yeah. It was actually my first day ever teaching. I had all the credits and practice semesters, but I've never had my own classroom," she replied.

"Really? What were you doing with all that education then if you weren't teaching?"

Not a damn thing, she thought bitterly. All the time she'd wasted could have been time spent helping kids, but that wasn't an answer she wanted to give to Mark. "I was getting my Masters degree and considering med school. I got the degree, but decided teaching was the better choice for me."

He nodded and turned at an intersection. "Yeah? That's great. And it works out well for the school too. I always like when they hire hometown people. It's good for the kids to see someone who's been in their shoes make something of themselves, and then come back and share their gifts."

Ben nodded at his thoughtful words. It was something she'd been told a few times by school board members and fellow staff, and it had made the transition sweeter. No one she'd spoke with regretted coming home, and she didn't think she would either.

"I'm glad to be back."

When Mark took a second at a stop sign to turn and smile at her she smiled back. He went back to driving, and she missed the joy his expression had shared but they were nearly to her place. It was probably best she didn't get addicted to his presence.

"I'm on the north side of the building."

The car driving in front of them turned onto a side road. Nothing about the vehicle stood out, but when the driver was in sight for a split second Ben gasped.

"Whoa, all right there, Ben?"

She wasn't all right. If the driver was who she suspected, Ben was a long way from okay.

"Um, I'm fine."

"Are you sure? Did you know someone in that car? I think she waved," Mark said, and Ben fought the urge to jump out of the truck and run to the safety of her apartment.

"No, I didn't know her." Ben looked between the windshield and rearview mirror as Mark pulled the truck to the curb. She didn't know if the car would return or not, but if it did she had to be ready to run.

"I can try to catch her if you want," Mark offered.

Her stomach turned at his words. "No, God, no. Why would you do that?" She grabbed her grocery bags in one hand and jumped out of the truck before she said something more. "Thanks for the ride."

"Hey, no problem," he called. "Is everything okay, Ben?"

She waved but didn't look back as she made a beeline for the building. She had to get inside.

The renovated Victorian house had homie touches like the front porch and shared hallways Ben liked aesthetically, and for safety sake, they provided an openness that made it difficult for intruders to hide. Ideally she would have moved into a second or third floor apartment, but only the lower front had been available. After she'd found out her husband hadn't been killed randomly, those things had become important.

He'd been murdered by a woman he'd been seeing for over a year. Ben had never met her, had never known about her, until the police had shown her pictures. When she'd begun to get frightening messages in Chicago, she'd known it was time to go home.

Ben vaulted up the porch stairs and closed the main door behind her, telling herself she was overreacting. She walked to her door and blew out a relived breath when she found it locked as she'd left it. The police in Chicago had told her not to worry, and she tried to follow their advice. That didn't stop her from triple locking her door.

Chapter 4

The calls started at dusk. Ben looked at the phone and waited. It could be anyone, but she knew it wasn't. Only one person called her at dusk. She chewed her thumbnail, a horrible habit she'd broken years ago, but it was back. Just like the harassment.

She considered not answering the phone or just turning it off, but Ben knew it wouldn't work. If she didn't answer, rocks started coming through her window, or worse. Ben didn't think she could handle worse again. The door was locked and had the chair in front of it. Her bedroom was also bolted shut. The windows were locked, and all the shades were drawn. Her world was as small and protected as Ben could make it. All but the phone. The new number didn't matter, and the fact that it was unlisted seemed like no deterrent at all against her stalker.

The phone rang again. Ben tasted blood on her lip and realized she'd bitten through the skin on her thumb. She wiped her abused nail with a tissue and lifted the receiver to her ear.

"Leave me alone, please, leave me alone." She was begging. She needed peace and if begging was what her stalker wanted, she'd push aside her pride and do it. "I'd give you money if I had any. Please, just tell me what I can do to get this to stop."

"I don't want your money, Bennie. Don gave me plenty." The voice. It wasn't often that the woman actually spoke, but every time it gave Ben chills. There was something wrong with the woman. Something evil.

"Then what? Please. I want this over."

"Oh. I don't know, Bennie, there's so much." She laughed, a nearly sweet giggle that made her sound like she was flirting, and Ben cringed. Between the front door lock and the bolt on her bedroom door only feet away, she was safe. She knew that, but the knowledge didn't stop her from shaking.

"What do you want from me?" she demanded again, checking the windows.

"I watched you at the funeral, and you cried and I liked that. I want you to cry while I watch. I want to taste your tears."

"I've cried," Ben confessed, the tears threatening again as helplessness filled her. "All the time."

"Good, then you're doing something right," the stalker replied, the bubbling flirt so strong in her twisted words Ben felt dirty just listening. "Don't worry, by the time I'm done with you those itty bitty tears will be the least of your worries. You just wait and see."

The line went dead again, but Ben didn't let go of the receiver for a long moment. She stared at the phone and at her bedroom door, straining to hear if there was movement in the rest of her apartment. She was going crazy.

But this time she wasn't running. She had nowhere to run. She set her phone beside the cradle and pulled her cellphone from her nightstand. It was a pay-by-the-minute plan and wickedly expensive, but in Chicago the police had used her hanging up the phone as a reason not to pursue the threatening phone calls.

Ben turned on her cellphone. She'd made enough mistakes to know if she started making them again she'd be dead. As much as she didn't want to bring anyone into her problems, she couldn't handle them herself. Praying for patience and for the help she so desperately needed, she dialed nine-one-one.

* * * *

Ben didn't know how she was going to stay awake. Her normally uncomfortable stool at her desk was worse than usual, but that still didn't keep her eyes from drooping.

After calling the sheriff, she'd agreed to go down to the station to give the full details while an officer looked over her apartment. She'd gone over all the sordid details of her past with the sheriff and one of his deputies. The ugliness was all Don's and, unlike in Chicago, the Flathead Falls police left the blame on him and let her be the victim.

In Chicago, superficial attempts had been made to catch Don's killer, but in the police's eyes, Victoria had done them a favor in gunning Don down. Ben shivered when she remembered one of the detectives telling her that word for word. They had never, and would never, waste manpower to chase down a woman who had done a public service.

Asleep on her feet, Ben finished her attendance papers and locked her classroom door at four o'clock. The sheriff had advised against walking alone after dark, but since it was still early fall, she had a few more weeks until she really needed to use her car. Ben waved to a deputy as he made a drive past her apartment complex just like the sheriff promised.

Hope filled her for the first time in months.

She was about to stop at home when she remembered her aunt had asked her to drop by the nursing home and say 'hi' to one of her old friends.

Ben never minded doing her aunt's bidding, especially if it meant Whilemina Riggs would stay out of her everyday life a little longer. She smiled as she turned toward the nursing home. The good thing about small towns was the distance between places, and of course, the fact that her aunt had sworn never to live in one again.

She loved her aunt, she really did, but the elder Riggs was a pill and a half. Ben turned onto the path leading to the nursing home. She'd visited often with church groups throughout the years and mentally added it to places to escape to when the evenings in her little apartment got too long.

A honk came from behind her. She froze, but after she turned and saw who it was, she smiled. Deputy Teddy Williams, the one who answered her call the night before, had kept an eye on her. He waved as he passed. The hope that had started to bubble became something more and she felt safe. It was so foreign it made her feel a little giddy.

She walked to the front desk and smiled when the receptionist gave her a puzzled look. Ben toned down the wattage on her smile when the other woman showed no signs of warming up.

"Hi, I'm here to see Mable Hampton."

"You must be Ben." A nurse from behind the desk shuffled paperwork before she finally looked up. "Mable is already sleeping for the night. She had a tough day."

"Oh, I'm so sorry to hear that," Ben replied.

"But I'll let your aunt know you did indeed come by," the nurse said with a smirk.

"She's called?"

"Four times," she answered, and Ben enjoyed the bit of camaraderie that she wasn't the only one her aunt drove crazy. "I'll let her know you stopped by, and if you would like to see Mable, and she's a dear so you'll both enjoy it, Thursdays are usually better."

Ben swung her tote higher on her back and nodded. "Okay, I'll try back on Thursday. Thanks."

She had time she didn't know what she was going to do with, but suddenly that didn't seem like such a bad thing. With a lighter heart she headed back into the heat. The building was surrounded by gardens with paths, so she picked one and strolled through the flowers. If she came across one of the residents, well maybe she could visit with them for a while. Otherwise it was just nice to be in the quiet, surrounded by pretty things.

When she came to a fork in the path, she took a long moment to decide her next direction. Finally, she took a side path and was thrilled when it narrowed slightly and ended at a fountain. Unfortunately, the sweet trickling of water didn't meet her ears as it should have. She stopped short when a denim-covered butt under one of the electrical panels caught her eye. It was a little naughty, but as she quietly ogled, she couldn't help but think it was familiar.

The left pocket was torn, allowing a bit of white from beneath to show. The shoes were nondescript, but very white. So familiar, but she couldn't put her finger on who it was until she saw the baseball cap lying beside him with a few tools. Feeling freer than she had in months, she grinned.

"Wow, the scenery around here sure has improved since the last time I visited."

He jerked hard and when the blunted sound of his head connecting with the metal box rang out she winced even as she bit back a giggle. She stepped into the landscape and offered Mark Dougstat a hand when he shimmied out, his palm pressed to his forehead.

"Are you okay?" she asked, checking for blood in case he'd really hurt himself.

He peeked from beneath his hand, and pink tinged his cheeks. "Um, yeah, I'm fine. Just rung my bell a little."

"I bet." She bit her cheek to stop her inappropriate laughter. She felt giddy, though, at being so bold and carefree with a man. "I should have given you a little more warning. Sorry about that."

"No problem," he said and stood up without taking her hand. A small red abrasion showed on his forehead, but other than the scrape he looked fine.

More than fine, Ben thought, looking him up and down as he reached to the ground for his hat. Mark Dougstat was a handsome man. Older than her usual type, if she even had one anymore. She didn't even want to think about her lack of dating skills. Instead she smiled again and just let herself enjoy Mark smiling back at her.

"So, you volunteer for the school board and here too? What don't you do, Mr. Dougstat?"

He flushed again, like he was embarrassed by the praise, which Ben found all the more endearing.

"I help out with maintenance here, along with a few of the other men from my church. The nursing home had to cut one of the maintenance positions because of cost this year, so we're stepping in when we can," he explained.

He was too good to be true, Ben thought as he pulled a handkerchief from his pocket and dusted his hands off. Or maybe it had just been too long since she'd been around a man who wasn't scum. She worried the latter was true, but at the moment that past didn't matter.

"And what are you doing here, Ms. Riggs?" Mark asked, his tone playful. "Doing a little catching up?"

"I tried to. One of my aunt's friends lives here, but Mable is snoozing so I'll be back Thursday." She tried not fidget under his gaze.

She felt his focus solely on her, and that wasn't something she was accustomed to. Even in class when everyone was supposed to be paying attention, she knew they didn't. Mark's gaze didn't waver, and she felt like she was the only one in his world.

"That's nice." He nodded. "It's great that you're jumping right back into Flathead Falls."

"Yeah, I think so," she replied.

"I suppose you walked again?" he asked, maintaining eye contact even as he gathered up the tools and plastic covered manual beside him.

"I sure did. I thought I might as well make the most of this Indian summer we're having."

He nodded again, and she loved how expressive he was. With Mark, she didn't have to look deeper because she didn't think there was a next layer on him; he was just a genuinely caring, playful man. Simple in the best way.

"I'm through here for now. Can I give you a ride home?" he asked.

"Are you sure I wouldn't be out of your way?" she replied, watching his eyes light up at the slight flirt in her voice. It was so nice to tease.

"Darlin' the city is twenty blocks total." His voice was all smooth southern drawl and sexy. A shiver ran up her spine as he winked. "And nothing is out of the way when it comes to helping a pretty woman."

Ten minutes later, Ben watched as Mark pulled away from the apartment building's curb. He was so sweet. They'd laughed through the short drive. The entire time they'd sat and cracked each other up, and she'd had the strongest urge just to hold his hand.

She adjusted her backpack and headed into the apartment, looking briefly at the front window when she remembered wanting a window planter. She made a mental note to talk to the superintendent about it soon. Maybe Mark could help her put something together. He was awful handy.

What would an hour with him be like? She wondered how quickly holding hands would progress with a man like him. He'd mentioned church a few times and she also had a strong faith, so that made her think he'd court low and slow. Courting, an old word, but as Ben turned her key in the door lock, she thought it suited Mark.

She flipped on the light switch and the bubbly, bemused feelings she'd indulged most of the day evaporated. An envelope waited on the floor with her name written in elaborate cursive. Ben didn't lean down or bother to pick it up. She retraced her steps until she returned to the front porch, then pulled out her cellphone and called it in.

* * * *

"Uncle Mark, can I eat the chocolate ice cream?"

Mark swore as the interruption made him jump, his niece breaking his concentration. Thankfully the jerk hadn't done any damage to the birdhouse or to his fingers. He unplugged the saw and leaned back from the bench.

"What chocolate ice cream, Kira? I bought vanilla."

"It's double chocolate chip, and it looks good," she called, and his memory clicked.

"Ah, wait up, kiddo. I don't think that's ours." He set the birdhouse higher on the counter so it wouldn't fall and headed into the house.

The place was a mess, papers strategically placed all over, dishes in the sink, and the floor needed to be swept. With school starting and the hay needing close attention, who had the time?

He liked things to be neat and tidy but not enough to spend his whole damn day working at it. When the weather was nice and there were chores to be done, inside the house was the last place he wanted to be. He'd clean in the winter when he was stuck for hours on end and the kids were in school.

"Who else would have ice cream in the freezer?" Kira demanded, standing up straight from where she'd been bent over the open chest freezer on the front porch.

She was out of her school clothes and into cutoff jean shorts and a yellow half t-shirt she called a baby-t. He didn't complain, not yet anyway. He figured he'd save it for a few years down the road when that sort of shirt meant something more than his little girl was hot and the air conditioner was acting up.

"Well, I think it belongs to Ms. Riggs, Thomas's chemistry teacher." Mark plucked the box from her hand and looped the other ice cream tub's red handle over her skinny wrist instead. "I gave her a ride home the other night and she must have forgotten it, so paws off, squirt."

"Uncle Mark, you're so weird." Her tone was a little sassy, but she stopped short of rolling her eyes.

He was glad her manners were finally coming back. Since she'd come home from France, she'd been an eye-rolling, back-talking little heathen. It had taken a few bouts of chair guarding in the corner, but she'd straightened up relatively quickly and was back to being the girl he'd raised.

He walked through the kitchen and to the living room. The air conditioner hummed and did its job in the little space, but it was days like this that made him want to put in central air. It was on the to-do list right after finishing the basement and putting in a new chicken coop.

"Hey, Thomas?" Mark called up the stairs. The narrow staircase was more humid than the other rooms put together, but Thomas still preferred to do his homework in his room rather than at the table like he had as a kid.

"Yeah?"

"Where's the paper your chemistry teacher sent home?" he asked.

"What do you need?" The squeak from Thomas's office chair announced he was moving for the request.

"Ms. Riggs's phone number. I gave her a ride, and she forgot her ice cream."

Thomas's tall, lanky frame nearly filled the narrow enclave of the staircase. He bypassed his sister's side room and hung from the pull-up bar he'd begged for years ago. "Here you go. Ice cream, huh? Are you sure you don't like her or something?"

"What? No, well she's cute, but she had a couple of bags the other day at the store, so I gave her a ride to her apartment."

"I heard you gave her a ride yesterday too," Thomas said with a smirk.

The joys of living in a small town, Mark thought as he reached for the paper only to have Thomas snatch it back. "She'd gone to visit someone at the nursing home, and we both finished up at the same time," Mark explained.

"Riigghhtt. Did you know she's a widow?" Thomas asked, still holding the paper out of his reach.

"Which means she's single and I don't have to fight her off with a stick when she jumps me for bringing her ice cream to her house." Mark hoped he sounded sarcastic, because the comment she'd made about his butt still crept into his thoughts more than occasionally. "Come on, I just met the woman and honest to God, how many women have I brought home?"

"We aren't here in the summer," Thomas pointed out.

"That's true, and even when you're nowhere in sight I still strike out. It's as if the scent of a hormonal, cranky teenager and one right on the cusp of adolescence hangs in the air, and acts like chick repellant."

Mark had missed the back-and-forth with Thomas. The boy was smart and a joy to be around.

He adored his niece and nephew, but the situation was complicated. That made any serious talk or thoughts of Ben something that required much more time than he'd given it. He wasn't about to bring in a woman who wouldn't understand, and frankly he didn't have the time to date.

"Yeah, like the cow poop isn't enough to keep the women away," Thomas teased right back and finally handed over the paper. "Do me a big favor and don't knock her up your first time out. All the guys like her as a teacher, and you know babies make chicks crazy."

"Who tells you this stuff?" Mark demanded, laughing out loud. "I'm going to remember all of this crap for your wedding toast in ten years, and it's gonna be a doozy."

Thomas laughed back, the threat an old one but a good one. So far Mark had potty training, little league, puberty and early thoughts on the opposite sex as speech fodder.

He left Thomas to finish his homework and headed to the kitchen. He grabbed the old phone hanging on the wall and pulled it to his office slash laundry room, the cord long enough for him to sit at his messy desk with it. He probably should have bought a cordless one years ago, but he liked his old trusty one that worked even when the power was out and never had to be recharged.

"Leave me alone! I've talked to the police here, and they will find you, so just leave!"

"Whoa, Ben?" The dial tone was back before he got a reply. He dialed again and the call was answered on the first ring. "Hello?"

"Who is this?"

"This is Mark Dougstat." He was careful to talk slowly so she understood in case something was wrong. "You left some ice cream in my truck, and we just found it. I was going to ask when would be a good time to bring it by?"

"Oh, sweet Jesus, Mark, I'm sorry. I've had some prank phone calls spook me a little, and I overreacted. I'm so sorry."

"No problem, honey," he assured her, though the news disturbed him. "A woman living alone in a new city, even if it's an old one, has to be careful. You've called the sheriff?"

"Yes, he's looking into it since they've been threatening. So ice cream, huh? I was wondering what had happened to it. I can pick it up. I mean, you've driven plenty on my behalf."

"No, don't worry about that. I have to run into town tonight for a meeting. Dropping by won't be a problem if you're going to be home." He was already putting on his fresh sneakers, the urge to get to her and make sure she was okay overwhelming.

"Okay, if you're sure you don't mind, I'll be here."

"See you in about twenty minutes?" he offered.

"Sure, drive safe."

Mark was torn between concern and a smile as he walked to the kitchen and hung up. Thomas sat with his sister at the table, both with big bowls of ice cream swimming in chocolate sauce. How those kids stayed so skinny he didn't know, but his mom said the same about him when he was Thomas's age.

"Going to see Ms. Riggs?" Thomas asked, and Kira snickered.

"Come on, guys, I just met her. I'm actually just going to stop by for a few minutes before I go to my AA meeting at church." He smacked his dusty hat against his jeans as he dodged the question.

"Sure you've got your meeting, but first you're going to bring her ice cream and play kissy face and make baby Uncle Marks." Kira giggled, elbowing her brother in a comradely way.

"Doubt it. She'll shoot him down right after he delivers the ice cream and send him packing, so she can wash her hair or check her Facebook page," Thomas predicted. "Then he'll be back to sweet talking the cows. How's Rowena doing?"

"One of these days," Mark muttered as he grabbed his keys, "the circus is going to come around, and I'm selling both of you to it. Thomas, watch your sister. Both of you take showers, and I'll call on my way home."

The kids laughed, and Mark smiled at the sound as he headed out the door. Their laughter meant something to him. Something he couldn't explain. From the first time he'd held Thomas, a wiggly, curious three year old, he'd been in love. The little guy had joined him most days, because Mark's mom needed a break from the constant duties of caring for her grandchild.

The memory made Mark's jaw tighten as he started up his truck and rolled down the windows. His sister wasn't going to win any parenting prizes, that was for sure. Maybe in science, but as far as Mark was concerned she'd dropped the ball with her kids. With the exception of the time immediately following Mark's father's death, Mark had taken care of Thomas and Kira, and he had every intention of finishing the job with them.

He pulled up to the curb in front of Ben's apartment and waved to Steven Redick as he drove by in his latest piece of junk car. That guy was bad news but an old friend. There had been a time Steven had helped him drown some sorrows.

After finding his father crushed beneath a tractor, Mark had let his demons find him and hit alcohol too hard. He'd cleaned up his act after Thomas called him from Paris in tears about his new baby sister not liking her nanny. When the little boy had begged to come "home" Mark had straightened himself up and asked for help.

Almost ten years sober and just thinking about that time made his insides turn cold. It was good he was heading to a meeting tonight. It hadn't been too long since he'd reaffirmed his commitment to sobriety, but it had been long enough.

He shrugged off the hard thoughts as he headed up the sidewalk for Ben's apartment, ice cream in hand. There was a line between remembering and learning from the past and living in it. God was always opening new windows, and Mark wasn't going to miss them by not looking.

The main apartment door opened before he made it to the top of the stairs. He smiled, wondering if God was switching to opening doors for him instead. The thought faltered when he saw Ben. He'd seen her less than twenty-four hours earlier, but she looked ten years older. Her skin was pale, bags were beneath her eyes, and though she tried to smile, he saw right through it.

The phone calls, he remembered. They must have been giving her more of a hard time than he thought.

"Hi." He smiled and offered her the ice cream. He wanted to hug her and tell her everything was okay. Something made him need Ben to be all right.

"Thanks," she said and forced a smile. "Um, do you have time for a pop or something?"

From the way she'd completely closed in on herself, he thought she didn't really want him to accept. He had the time though, and his curiosity was piqued.

"Sure, that would be great."

She might not want him there, but he had to know what was going on and if he could help. He felt a burst of pride when she opened the main door and motioned him in. He was too emotionally involved with Ben considering their short acquaintance, but even knowing that wasn't enough to put a cap on what he felt.

He followed her through the hall to her apartment as she apologized for the mess he didn't notice at all. Papers sat in neat stacks on the table, but not much else. What he did notice was the lack of...everything.

There was a sagging couch with no pillows or throws, a tiny TV that looked older than he and Ben combined, and a cheap coffee table. That was all except the microscopic kitchen, where only a table and two chairs sat. The doorless top cabinets showed less than a four person set of mismatched dishes.

"I'm still working on getting things the way I like them," Ben explained, putting the ice cream in a freezer, which, he saw held only ice cube trays.

"I see." He watched as she pulled out a jug of store brand pop and two glasses. "You were in Chicago, right?"

"Yes. I went to the University of Illinois in Chicago. It's a great school, and I liked it a lot. They have an intense chemistry program."

"I never made it out of Flathead Falls. My dad and mom helped me buy my place when I turned twenty-three, then with the kids I just never got anywhere else," he replied and took a seat after she did. He wanted to make her comfortable because she looked ready to jump out of her skin. Such tension...he hadn't seen someone so on edge in a long time.

"Well, if you had to choose a place, Flathead Falls is a nice one." She smiled, not judging or condescending, just friendly he thought.

She passed him a glass of pop and took a sip of hers. She was still nervous, even if her hands weren't shaking as badly as they had been earlier. Looking around Ben's tiny home though, he couldn't help but make comparisons and follow leads he didn't like.

There had to be an ugly reason for her living as she was. Curiosity already piqued from chatting with her before, every meeting he found himself being drawn deeper into her life. He wondered if the circumstances surrounding her deceased husband had anything to do with the modest way she lived.

"Say, you don't want to grab some dinner, do you?" he asked.

She had no food in her freezer, and he'd bet what she'd bought the other day was all she had in her cupboards. That was unacceptable. It might make him late for the meeting, but he had to be sure she was all right.

"I actually had a dinner meeting at school," she explained, and he wondered if she was lying. Pride could be an ugly and restrictive emotion. "But thanks for asking."

"Of course," he replied. If she was lying, he wasn't going to call her on it. Not yet anyway. He wanted more answers, and alienating her wasn't going to help.

The phone rang and Ben jumped to her feet. Any color that their discussion had put on her face faded. She looked at him then at the phone with panicked eyes. She was a troubled woman, and Mark hated it.

"Want me to get it?"

"No, but um, I should, or they won't stop." Her teeth showed wide in the forced smile, a look he'd taken pride in not seeing for the last few minutes. "Excuse me a second?"

The tiny apartment gave no hope for privacy, so he sat at the table and waited while she lifted the receiver with a trembling hand.

"Hello."

She stayed on the line for a minute, paling even farther while she pulled and rubbed her dark curls just above her ear. Finally, she hung up none too gently and turned back to him with a shaky smile. "Sorry about that. So how's the football team going to do this year?"

He didn't want to let her steer the conversation away from herself, but since he was trespassing on her territory, he let her. He knew fear, had seen it before, had felt it to his core, and he was looking at it again.

They spoke of mundane things, of the town and his farm and the football team. She started to relax, but when the time pressed close to an hour she started fidgeting with her glass again.

"Didn't you say you had a meeting tonight?" she asked when the hour was nearly upon them.

She was right, but there had to be a reason she was running him off, and he didn't like it. If she was left alone…hell, it felt wrong to leave her alone. He shook himself. Their short acquaintance didn't warrant such protectiveness. "Yeah, I suppose I should go. It's been nice getting to know you, Ben."

"Thanks, you too."

"We could do this again soon," he offered. "Maybe get to a movie, dinner?"

Stephanie Beck

"That is the nicest offer I've had in months, and thanks." Her smile was sad. "Really, but I don't think I'm ready for movies or dinners with nice men. I'm still getting used to being a widow."

He could have kicked himself. Maybe that was one of the reasons she was so uncomfortable. He'd thought they'd flirted a bit the night before, but she might have only been trying her wings. "I knew that. I'm sorry. That was inappropriate."

"No, not at all." She shook her head firmly. "No, it's not the widowhood I'm getting accustomed to. It's more the fact Don was killed by his mistress and left me in a ton of debt. It's not you, it's me, and I have a lot of issues right now."

"Hell." So much more about the night and her life made sense, even if it wasn't sense he liked. "Are you serious?"

She rubbed her palm hard against her forehead and wouldn't meet his eyes. "Damn. I must be more tired than I thought to have said that. I'm sorry. It's… Let's just forget that, okay?"

"All right. You've got a lot on your plate right now, I understand. If you are ever in the mood for a movie or dinner, you've got my number. We can keep things friendly and casual if it makes you feel more comfortable. We could bring the kids along. I can always use another set of eyes when wrangling the kids, and an ally when it comes to choosing a movie that doesn't feature pre-teens singing and dancing. Friends are good, right?"

"Definitely." Her smile was less forced but when she shook his offered hand, her palm was cold, colder than it should have been in the heat. She was looking toward the clock again too. "Thanks for bringing back my ice cream."

"My pleasure," he replied. "And really, don't hesitate to call me. I'm awake late and up early. Plus, I spend most of my time with cows and kids, so I always enjoy the chance to have a conversation with another adult."

"Okay, that's got to be the second nicest offer I've had today." Ben laughed and walked him the three steps to her door. "Drive safe."

"Yeah, and hey, you should call the sheriff again if those phone calls keep up." The advice probably wasn't necessary, but he couldn't stop himself from caring. "It's his job to take care of pricks like that."

"I'll remember that." She closed the door before he'd turned.

Ben Riggs was a troubled woman, he thought, taking a moment to let his eyes accustom to the darker entry hall. The tiny apartment and shadowed eyes made much more sense since her slip. Those kinds of closeted issues only led to more trouble.

Mark took a step and paused. He wasn't sure, but he thought he heard the phone ring again; right after a chair had been slid under the door.

Chapter 5

"Ben, thank God."

She frowned at her school telephone receiver, and for the life of her, she couldn't figure out who was on the other end of the line. Her study hall period had just started, a half a dozen upperclassmen working on homework diligently in the fifth week of class.

To tell the truth, she needed the quiet. Between getting her finances in order and the harassment, her nerves were shot. She could handle the debt. She accepted it as the unfair but unavoidable price she had to pay for being obliviously happy those six years.

It was the stalker who was wearing on her. The calls continued, photos of Ben walking to school had been stuffed under her door, and twice someone had thrown rocks at her bedroom window at two in the morning. The sheriff was helping. He still had patrols in the area, and one of the deputies always seemed to be within five minutes of the building.

Something had to give, and she was afraid it was going to be her mind.

The phone in her hand reminded her the voice hadn't said anything more. Victoria hadn't employed outside tormentors yet, but Ben didn't discount the idea.

"May I help you?" She was terrified of what the next words would be.

"Hell, sorry. This is Mark Dougstat."

Ben sagged in relief.

"Mark, hello. It's nice to hear from you. Can I help you with something?" She hadn't seen him in a few weeks, and that was for the best. She liked him, but given what had happened to the last man she'd loved…distance was better.

"God, I hope so. Kira just got home. Kira, my niece?" He sounded desperate.

"Yes, I remember. She's nine, right?"

"Yeah, why the hell do nine year olds have these sorts of issues? She's nine, damn it. Her backup moms and their families are on vacation together in Hawaii, and she needs female stuff." She could hear him shudder across the phone. "I wouldn't have called, but it's an emergency and I'm out of women to call."

"Oh, okay." The trepidation from the initial call was replaced by curiosity and amusement. "She's having her period?"

"God no, the books said that wouldn't happen for a few years yet." Mark swore, and she bit back a laugh. She liked this side of Mark that wasn't so put together. Just as she'd liked the embarrassed Mark at the nursing home. "No, her teacher sent home this notice about undershirts, training bras and deodorant. Thomas stinks. I've got that covered and bought stock in the deodorant company, but what the hell do girls use? What exactly does a training bra train what to do?"

"Gotcha." She tried hard not to laugh as he sounded more and more frantic. "I'm sure those things are just suggestions."

"Yeah, but she's crying about it. It's important, and her two best friends are on vacation for another few days and all of a sudden she's gonna be the only girl without this stuff. Can you help? Do you have time tonight or this weekend to run to KC? I'll buy you dinner, movie, diamonds, whatever you want."

"I do like diamonds," she teased, her earlier hesitance to have anything to do with him eased because he needed help. "Any time works for me, Mark. I'm not busy at all this weekend, just church on Sunday."

"Thank you. Thank you. How about Saturday morning? We'll make the drive, hit a matinee, do some shopping, get dinner and make it back before chores."

"Works for me." She spent another minute talking with him and nailing down times, Mark thanking her every other sentence. He was so adorable. "Don't worry about it. I'm happy to help."

"I really do appreciate this, Ben. We'll see you tomorrow at ten." He sounded a little more at ease, the husky quality back to replace the panic.

"Great. Have a nice night."

When Ben locked up her room for the day, she sighed at how fast it had flown by. It was crazy, but she wished the days lasted longer. She dragged it out as long as she could, but if she stayed later than four thirty, she attracted attention. Sharing her problem had been hard enough with the sheriff, but since the stalker hadn't made any contact at school, Ben had been able to keep the issue to herself at work.

She was off the school block in only minutes despite dragging her feet. The only things left in the night were to finish her walk, eat dinner, grade papers and hope the calls didn't come.

Maybe she could spend more time at the nursing home or volunteering for church, she thought. But that opened the door for threats. If she got close to anyone, Ben knew in her gut they could be hurt. The possibilities were terrifying enough to make her maintain her lonely evenings. The trip with Mark and the kids to KC probably tempted fate, but she was weak and lonely and it was out of town.

She turned a sharp corner near the hardware store and was nearly knocked to the ground by an oversized man who must have been equally as distracted. "Oh, sorry, ma'am. You okay?"

"Yes, thanks." Shaken out of her thoughts, Ben offered a smile. "I need to pay more attention, I guess."

He nodded and kept walking, and she did the same, keeping a leisurely pace to her apartment. It was warm for October, and she would probably turn on her air conditioner until night came and cooled things off.

She was nearly home when she realized she needed to get to the bank if she planned on shopping. She might not need it, but she should at least be able to contribute for her movie ticket and meal. Besides, if there was a sale, she needed a pair of tennis shoes. She turned around and walked the three blocks back to town, pleased to have one more reason to delay the lonely night ahead.

* * * *

"What the hell? Where is she?" Victoria Maris slammed down the phone at five o'clock when it continued to ring. "I thought you said she would be home by now."

"She should be," Steven insisted. "I ran into her going by the hardware store. Even a chunky girl like her should be able to make it to the apartment building in less than ten minutes. Maybe she's on the can."

Victoria refused to dignify that with a response. Her vile cohort became less and less tolerable every day, and she hated having him in the same room.

His stench offended her, even when he tried to cover it with layers of his cheap cologne. Everything was getting on her nerves, but she knew it was the waiting. They were getting closer to the big day when Bennie would pay.

Ideally Victoria wanted to finish alone and be done with Steven altogether, but for a while longer at least, he had his uses.

"Go over there and find out what she's doing."

"It's too fucking hot, babe." When he wiped his pasty brow with the edge of his sweat yellowed shirttail Victoria thought she'd be ill. "Call her in an hour. Maybe she had to stop by the store or something."

Her jaw hurt from holding back her reply. She wanted to kill him. He was a moron and a pig, but he was familiar with the territory. If she wanted to kill Ben, and she did, that meant keeping him around a little longer.

"If you go I'll make you very happy tonight," Victoria offered, adding a seductive purr to her voice.

He scratched his belly and had the nerve to snort in disgust. "Yeah, then you'll get off like a whore in the bathroom. Cock not good enough for ya?"

"Yours is." She twisted just right as she stood, showing the high tops of her thighs as she managed to also pull her v-neck down a bit. There was a reason she kept him around, and she expected him to do his job but understood him enough to know he needed a little incentive. "But that doesn't mean I don't like to play with myself. You certainly like to play with me."

"Yeah, I guess." His eyes locked to her breasts. The filthy lust in his gaze would have made a lesser woman squirm, but Victoria knew exactly what she was doing. The price Steven exacted with his lackluster desires fit well within the range she was willing to pay to get her way. "I love those tits of yours. Lift your shirt."

"Oh, I'll do a whole lot more if you'll go see if Bennie is home yet," she replied, tugging her shirt up her rib cage. "All this heat and humidity is making me sticky. Maybe you'd like to join me in the bathtub tonight?"

"Like we'd both fit." He tilted his head, still staring, and Victoria knew she was only a few promises from getting her way.

"Then I'll go in and you can watch, silly." She added a little giggle for good measure. He loved the dirty schoolgirl routine, and she wanted him to move. "When I'm done doing all those naughty things, you might have to punish me."

"It is naughty." The gleam of sexual mischief in his eyes, along with a little hint of meanness, perversely turned her on. "Maybe you'll need me to spank that ass and ream you good. That'll teach you not to be doing that shit."

"Maybe," she agreed, touching her breasts through her shirt because, fat pig or not, the idea of getting off in the bath with him watching and then being spanked and fucked really did it for her. "But I can't even think about it unless my work is done. You know how important my work is, Steven."

"Fuck." He hefted himself up, stalking toward her, and for a moment she thought he might just bend her over and take her. She wouldn't have hated it, either.

Of course she would have had to kill him for it later. But instead of screwing her raw, he grabbed her breasts harshly, squeezed once, and headed for the door. "I'll be back, and when I get here you'd better be naked and finger fucking yourself in that asshole of yours or I'm liable to break it."

"Whatever you say, Steven," she said sweetly. "Hurry."

Chapter 6

Ben was grateful she taught high school students. The whip-slim redhead beside her couldn't be sweeter and her intellect surpassed most kids her age, but she hadn't stopped talking since they'd met that morning. Ben didn't know how much more she could take.

So far, Kira had talked about school, the farm, her dog, her cows, her suspected lactose intolerance, and her toenail polish. There'd been a brief quiet during the movie, but the second the credits had rolled she'd been back talking about her undying adoration for Zac Efron.

Now she was talking about her friends. Ben tried not to be obvious as she looked frantically around Sears for the girls department. She really liked Kira, but if the little girl said 'like' one more time Ben thought she might cry.

"So Misty Mae totally has boobs already, and she had her period over the summer," Kira informed her as they walked by Hannah Montana adorned packs of underwear. "While I was in stupid France with a baby nanny she was becoming a real woman. I'm so jealous, 'cause I don't think I'll ever have boobs. My mom doesn't, and Grandma doesn't count 'cause she's old and they eventually just stretch and roll, right? Are yours stretched and rolled, Ben, or are they, like, real still?"

"Good Lord, girl, what are you talking about?" She laughed so hard at the earnest question she had to stop herself before she fell into a child-sized mannequin. She gasped until she finally caught her breath and could speak. "Rolled? No, mine are not rolled anywhere, and I have to say as a girl who developed early and just kept going, big breasts aren't everything."

"But aren't they, like, awesome?" Kira's face squished in confusion. "They mean you're mature and stuff."

"Maturity is a state of mind, but don't worry, kiddo, you've got lots of time. Now, are we looking for undershirts or training bras?"

Ben helped pick out half a dozen training bras and a two-pack of undershirts for the winter months ahead, as well as a new pack of underwear while they were at it. Apparently, Mark had bought her Dora the Explorer underwear when he went school shopping while Kira was in France, and that was unacceptable for someone of her advanced tastes.

Kira was still talking, and at the little girl's request, their purchases were safely out of sight in a paper bag as they walked from the store. Ben thought Kira was adorable and remembered doing the same thing with her aunt. Unfortunately, cute undies had been a waste according to her aunt, and because Ben had developed breasts a little early, her aunt had had to spend money sooner and made sure Ben had known it.

Thomas and Mark waited at the ball cap store. Thomas had a new Chief's hat, but his uncle's dusty, old Flathead Falls Frogs cap was still firmly on his own head. Constancy. Ben liked that about Mark.

He'd gotten a haircut since the last time he'd been to her apartment. He was a handsome guy, tall, broad and though his middle showed signs of softening a little with age, he looked good. Nearly forty, according to Kira, he was a strong man in his prime. More and more Ben had to remind herself she didn't need one of those.

She might like Mark, and the more she was around him the more she did, but she had a psychotic bitch stalking her who might just like to kill her. She couldn't let that spill onto him, and if they became more than casual friends she was afraid it would.

"Get everything you needed?" Mark looked like a kid hoping for presents on Christmas morning. Ben thought his desperation was the cutest thing she'd seen since watching Kira debate underpants.

"Yeah, Uncle Mark, we got everything," Kira assured him and handed over his debit card. "Thank you for buying me the clothes and for asking Ben to help."

"You're welcome, squirt. You know I would've done it if I'd had to. But I'm glad I didn't." The relief in his words made Ben smile. "So where else should we go? I think it's a little early for supper unless you guys are hungry?"

"Naw, I'm good from the popcorn still." Thomas readjusted his new hat and bent the stiff brim to curve it. "A cheeseburger would be good pretty soon. How about the shoe store at the other end?"

"Sounds fine with me," Ben replied when Mark looked to her.

They walked together, the two kids staying just in front. Thomas put a little distance between them as Kira went on chatting her brother's willing ear off. Ben hadn't had siblings or any family close to her age, and she was envious of their relationship. They were tight and didn't pick and fight with each other like so many siblings did. It was like they understood they were in their lives together and clung to one another. The time they spent in France sounded like it wasn't always the best, and Ben figured they were probably the only comfort the other had.

It was a sad situation, but they would have a special relationship because of it. Thomas would never let Kira be hurt and if she ever were, he would be there. Mark would be there too, of course, to help pick up the pieces. And Ben knew, as the little sister, Kira would key the car of the first girl to break Thomas's heart.

"Oh, a baby store! Come on, Ben, let's go see the baby stuff." Kira fell back from her place beside her brother to tug Ben into the brightly lit, happily colored store full of little clothes. "There were tons of cute clothes stores in Paris, but Mom said they were a waste of time so I didn't get to go to any. My dolly seriously needs some new clothes. Uncle Mark always rolls his eyes, and Thomas won't even come in with me anymore. Boys are so silly."

"They are." Ben started breaking out in hives the second she was surrounded by the beautiful little things.

"This would fit my dolly." Kira held up a preemie sun suit for inspection Ben turned to Mark who'd followed them in and bit back a smile when he indeed rolled his eyes. "Please?"

"No way." He shook his head at the tiny clothing while Ben fought to breathe and prayed neither of them noticed. "We've had this talk before, squirt. You can buy all the baby stuff you want secondhand with your allowance, but you aren't buying new stuff for Maggie."

"Maggie's my doll with the horribly lacking wardrobe," Kira explained to Ben as she put back the polka-dotted suit. "I can still look though, right, Uncle Mark?"

"Sure, baby, nothing wrong with that," he agreed as Kira continued to pull Ben deeper into the store.

She'd wanted a baby. More than anything, she had wanted a little one of her own, but it hadn't happened. She and Don had never used protection, not from day one, because they'd been married and both wanted a big family. Two years into their marriage Ben started working on getting pregnant.

She'd made sure she had enough folic acid, started eating better, lost ten pounds, exercised more and had been in the best shape of her life. She'd gotten over-the-counter ovulation kits, read all the books, but nothing happened. Eventually, she and Don had seen a specialist.

Dr. Miller had done everything, but nothing had worked.

"Ben?" At Mark's question she realized she hadn't been paying attention, lost in dark thoughts. "You okay?"

He looked concerned, so she pasted on a smile to reassure him. His look didn't change so she added, "Yes, I'm fine. Thanks. Are we ready to go?"

"Come on, Uncle Mark, it's super cute and only a dollar," Kira whined, holding a sweet little sunhat in pink polka-dot seersucker. "I couldn't get it at a garage sale for that. Tell him, Ben. That's cheap."

"It is very reasonable." She didn't reach to touch the offered cap because she didn't need that sort of burn surrounded by people. Ben looked toward the exit and wanted to run, but she'd already told Mark enough of her secrets. This one didn't need to be given life to ruin their good day.

"Fine. I should have known another woman would mean spending more." Mark sighed theatrically but handed over two dollar bills. "Go ahead, squirt, but that's out of your five bucks this week."

"Okay, Uncle Mark. Thank you," Kira squealed and ran toward the clerk, stopping short after two steps. "Come on, Ben, it's easier to check out with a grown up. Otherwise the lady always asks a bunch of questions and it takes forever."

Ben was shocked she could laugh, but Kira's exasperation cut through her dark thoughts. With so many new and wonderful things in her life, Ben knew it was time let go of the past.

Next they headed to a family chain restaurant at the end of the mall. After scouring the menu and asking Ben's opinion on every entrée, Kira ordered macaroni and cheese off the kid's menu. Thomas rolled his eyes at his sister as he ordered a triple burger with fries, a salad and a fruit plate.

In fascination, Ben watched how they interacted and again wished she had more family. They were great together. They teased in a way her aunt had never been comfortable with. There had always been a reminder on the tip of her tongue assuring Ben she really wasn't a welcome addition to her life.

As Ben had gotten older her aunt had made it abundantly clear she was a burden. Kira and Thomas didn't seem to feel that way at all, and not once did their uncle say or do anything that might change their attitudes.

He was single, and he should have been doing what he wanted. As he tossed a straw wrapper at Kira, who giggled and tossed it back, Ben realized he was doing what he wanted.

She tried not to watch Thomas eat. He wasn't impolite, but it was just too much. Instead she ate and listened to Kira talk about the other things she'd wanted to do in France, but hadn't gotten the chance to. Out of the corner of her eye she saw Thomas reach for one of Mark's fries. Without even breaking away from nodding about Kira's monolog, Mark swatted his nephew's hand. Ben looked at Thomas and the youth just grinned.

She expected Mark to share his fries, but instead he scarfed down the last few on his plate. She was about to offer Thomas hers in case he was genuinely still hungry, but the waitress came and Mark ordered half a dozen desserts. From across the table, Mark winked at her and passed a piece of chocolate cheesecake before Thomas could devour it. She was more thoughtful than ever as she ate.

Back in the car with a two hour drive ahead of them and the sun setting, Ben was pleasantly tired. She'd only thought a few times of the troubles waiting at home. She refused to let the crazy woman ruin a perfectly nice day, and it really had been nice. Family outings weren't something she was familiar with, so as far as a first run, she thought she'd done pretty well.

When the quiet from the backseat continued, Ben looked over her shoulder and was shocked to find Kira sleeping. Ben checked the clock and realized it had only been ten minutes.

"She's out already?" Ben asked quietly.

"Yep, she's a really good sleeper, especially in the car. When she was really little and had colic and croup and all that baby garbage, we'd get her bundled up and go for a ride. Thomas would put on his headphones and crash out next to me, and we'd drive until she fell asleep. He might not fall asleep now, but headphones are always out for major car trips. Case in point."

She looked back and sure enough Thomas had his iPod ears in and his eyes closed. He wasn't pulling away from his little sister, who slept on his shoulder. They made a pretty sight to end the day. "They are such good kids, Mark. You have to be so proud."

"Hell, yeah. They're amazing. We have a lot of fun." His grin said more than his words could. "How long were you married?"

"Six years. Almost seven."

"No kids?" He winced. "Sorry. That's really not my business."

She shrugged. Questions were bound to come up, and she'd resigned herself to the fact Mark was the kind of person she wanted to share her thoughts with. Already she'd let loose on some of her major secrets and

Stephanie Beck

they felt safe with him. "It's a long drive home. And you can always ask, Mark, as long as I don't always have to answer."

"Sounds fair."

"And no, we didn't have kids. We tried for a few years, and then we did fertility testing. Things weren't right, so I had hormone drugs and in-vitro, but I rejected that within a few days." She was still shaky and shouldn't have said anything so soon after visiting a baby store. Her emotions were right on the surface, but the more time she spent with Mark, the more easily the surface cracked. "We were going to try it again when everything happened. So…no babies."

"I'm sorry."

"Hey, no worries. It probably was for the best." There was no more she wanted to add, so silence filled the car, disturbed only by the sounds of Kira's breathing.

His quiet sympathy was probably the reason she'd spilled. So far he hadn't treated her any differently for knowing bits of her past and that's what she was afraid of, being treated as pitiful or dumb for the past she wanted to put behind her. With Mark she didn't feel like a loser, though in some aspects, she had earned the moniker.

"How about you? Any little Marks running around the county?"

"Nope." He chuckled. "When the kids were small I got lots of attention from the local women, but I had little kids and two farms to take care of, so I didn't have the time or inclination to take care of a woman too. I wasn't up to it then, and now the kids aren't so little anymore. They're great, ya know? Awesome judges of character and can spot a fake a mile away."

"Your own little tramp detectors, huh?" She smirked when he laughed.

"Yeah, I guess," he agreed, turning down a county road to Flathead Falls. She wasn't ready for the day to end. Like the other times she'd ridden with Mark, she wished the ride would go forever. "So are we going to do this again, honey? Just you and me? I know you said you had some issues, but I don't want to have to wait until the next grocery, nursing home or underwear related emergency before I see you again."

"I want to say yes, I really do, but I just don't think so." Declining his invitation was hard, but the right thing to do. "But feel free to call me with underwear emergencies."

"You also said you were in a lot of debt. Don't worry about that. I'm not one of those rich farmers who have wheelbarrows full of money." He'd ignored her gentle let down so crazily that she laughed. "I'll even admit I lied about owning stock in Thomas's deodorant manufacturer, so there is no way I'd be able to offer you money anyway."

"It's not just that." It felt wonderful to find humor in the one situation she hadn't been able to squeeze any from. She'd gratefully remember his words the next time she took out her checkbook. "The money is part of it, but there's more and it's ugly."

"There is still a lot of ride yet," he pointed out.

She hadn't planned to tell him what was happening, because she didn't want to tell anyone. The story was personal but Mark--he didn't seem so much like a stranger anymore. He obviously wanted to at least be friends; something she knew from his earlier confessions wasn't an undertaking he did without thought. It seemed fair to let him understand and decide. He was too nice of a man, too much of a friend, to think she was casually blowing him off.

"I have a stalker. She followed me from Chicago, and she really doesn't like me," Ben explained, trying to stay as practical as possible. "She killed my husband, and I don't know if she wants to kill me or just drive me crazy. Either way, I'm not going to let her sickness spread because of me."

She'd said it so quickly she worried he might ask her to repeat it. When he stayed quiet for a long moment she realized he was thinking. She blew out a breath, some of her tension gone. Mark was a synthesizer, she knew that from their time together. She'd shared a lot in a short amount of time, and though his silence was disconcerting, it was also comforting in a strange way.

"You've told the sheriff about all of this?"

"Yes. He's been great. He has extra patrols for my neighborhood, and he's taken me seriously. In Chicago the police considered me one step above a criminal." Ben laughed to take some of the bitterness out of the admission, but her treatment in Don's hometown still burned.

"Why's that?"

"Because I had no clue what was happening, and they couldn't believe in six years of marriage I'd never noticed anything," she explained, feeling stupid all over again. "Maybe I should have, but he never brought that kind of stuff home."

"You had a good marriage?"

"We loved each other. I stayed in school, took lots of extra classes and took care of Don. I loved it." The same confusion she always experienced when she remembered the time welled. She still didn't fully understand where her world took its ugly turn. "It's a classic case of the wife knowing last, I guess."

Mark shook his head. "That's tough. I'm glad he wasn't abusive. Sometimes when right and wrong get skewed it leads to people hurting the ones they love. It sounds like even though he was a screwup he loved you. That's probably why it's so hard to come to terms with everything."

"Yeah, I think you're right." She was touched by his insight and kindness when he could have judged. Mark was a better man than Don could have ever been, but still Mark found the good.

They drove in silence for a while, the flat farmland around them peaceful and empty for the most part, the occasional barn and house sprouting up from the plains.

It was nice to be in Missouri and surrounded by life instead of concrete and steel. Not only were the fields still full of thriving energy, albeit at the end of its cycle, but the people felt more real, more alive than the super-cyber ones in the city. Homegrown boys and girls had their own quirks for sure, but they were genuine and they cared. Like Mark, who showed it every chance he got.

"Are you scared?" His question was quiet, meant only for her ears along the desolate stretch of road.

"Oh yeah," she admitted with a ragged sigh.

He nodded and she sank deeper into her seat, embarrassed by her confession, but not too much, because he wasn't going to laugh. She knew that. Her instincts screamed he was decent and wouldn't hurt a fly.

Admittedly those instincts weren't so great, but Mark was an open book with his decency and temperament. He'd taken in his sister's kids for years to raise and love. When his mother had needed him, he'd worked not only his own farm but hers as well in times when farming wasn't profitable. Those things said a lot to Ben and having spent the day with him and the kids she was pretty confident in her assessment.

"You call me if you get scared. I'll talk to you, come in if you need me to. Thomas mentioned the other teachers are really warming up to you, so call them. We can't help if we don't know, you know what I mean?"

"I do," she whispered because her throat was tight from being so overwhelmed by his concern. "And thank you for that."

"You'd do the same. I was terrified of undershirts, training bras and whatever else Kira needed. You helped." His self-depreciating smile helped her find the peace to smile back a little. "Let me help you."

"Okay, we'll see."

"No, say, 'I'll call you, Mark, if there's something I can't handle.'"

She sat up straighter in her seat. She liked the sentiment, but her independence in the past months demanded to be noted. "There's nothing I can't handle."

He sighed. "That's not what I mean. I know you can. What I'm talking about are those nights or evenings that get a little too long. On those nights you could call me if a friendly voice would help. That's all I meant."

She should have known that was what he meant, and immediately relented. "Okay, I can do that."

"I know you *can*. It's the *will* I hope you'll put into effect when you need to." Mark pulled up to her apartment building and put the car in park. "Want me to walk you in?"

"Ah, actually, there's Teddy." She grabbed her bag with her new shoes and her purse when the sheriff's deputy pulled up and got out of his car. "He'll walk me in, but thank you. Really. Thanks for everything, Mark."

"I'll hear from you soon? Even if it's just a phone call to let me know you're all right?"

She looked into his blue-gray eyes that were as earnest and kind as the first time she'd met him. He was a special man and his offers, simple as they seemed, meant a lot to her and she couldn't just walk away from them.

"Yeah, I think you might."

Chapter 7

Ben's fingers were a sticky mess of glue and cotton balls. Making a marshmallow costume had sounded so simple in theory. When she'd chatted with Kira, and later her fellow science teachers in the teacher's lounge, putting it together couldn't have seemed easier.

Kira was going to dress up as a marshmallow for Halloween. Ben decided to do the same after the science department chose to dress as food for their party. A costume appropriate for all of her Halloween plans fit into her budget.

She'd picked up a big sheet of cardboard to wrap into a cylinder around herself, but it hadn't been real enough. After another trip to the store, she'd found herself elbow deep in cotton balls, but the tiresome process was having the desired fluffy and delicious effect.

She loved Halloween, and with all the small town plans, family parties, hayrides, apple picking and pumpkin carving, she had the day filled. She was throwing herself into it all with abandon. Mark had asked her to help with pumpkin carving at the library the day before Halloween, and she was looking forward to that too.

Every time she saw Mark she liked him more, and over the last month and a half he'd butted into her life at least two times a week. She didn't want to be involved but more than once now she'd overheard her name connected with Mark's and she had to admit, she didn't hate it.

She was going to a party with them Sunday night for hayrides and apple cider. One of Kira's backup moms threw it every year, and though Kira had been the one to ask Ben to come, she had seen the mild challenge in Mark's eyes when she'd looked to him for confirmation. Pleasure had also been there when she'd agreed to go, as Kira's date, of course.

The man was going to wear her down, she thought as she smeared glue on another cotton ball. He never pushed her, but in his little ways he was eroding her every resistance. Since the phone calls had spaced out and the pictures stopped, Ben was thinking maybe it wouldn't be so bad to let herself fall a little.

She missed having a man in her life and having someone who loved her within reach at the end of the day. Oh, and the nights, they got so damn long in her empty double bed.

There wasn't shame in her enjoyment of sex. Even from her first night with Don, physical intimacy had always been good. There had never been anything 'wrong' or taboo between them. If he wanted something she gave, always willing to learn, and if she wanted something she couldn't quite explain he'd never once gotten impatient.

She wondered what kind of lover Mark would be. She dribbled a line of glue and smiled as she considered Mark's lover clues. It wasn't difficult to imagine him hard and hot above her, driving in playfully or intensely. Beyond that her imagination couldn't quite place him in her naughtier fantasies.

Would he be comfortable with cock rings, vibrators and anal beads, or would he be more insistent on standard missionary? What would he think if she rode him or smacked his ass or bit his neck?

Would he refuse to play or would he just give that look he had, daring her to do whatever she wanted. The thought of the look made her shiver, because, honest to God, it was hot. The dominant expression didn't lose its potency even as a memory.

The phone rang after another row was meticulously finished. Ben groaned, not sure she could answer with her hands covered with glue and cotton fluff. She checked the clock and since it wasn't on the hour like Victoria's calls usually were, it could be from anyone.

She looked at her fingers and then back to the ringing phone. It was going to get messy, but it could very well be Mark calling, and that made the cleanup even more worthwhile.

"Hello?"

She tucked the phone between her ear and shoulder while she snapped and scraped her fingers to remove the sticky fluff.

"Oh, you are home! I'm so very glad."

The voice made her flicking hands halt.

"I'm sorry I've been out of touch. I bet you were worried, weren't you? But don't fret, our game is far from over."

"Please, please leave me alone." Ben rubbed at her hand, taking the frustration out on the fabric of her jeans and the skin on her fingers.

"Ya know? No." Her shrill laugh made Ben pull the phone from her ear, and she jumped at a sound from her darkened bedroom. "Uh oh, Bennie. Who's there?"

Ben tried to hang up and dial the police, but with the other end occupied she couldn't. She dropped the phone and ran for her triple dead bolted door, but it was too late.

The noise had become a person, a large, heavy man with a pair of dark hose skewing his face. She wasn't going to make it out in time, she thought, panic consuming her. When his arms wrapped around her from behind Ben knew escape wasn't going to be an option unless she fought.

She screamed and kicked when he lifted her off her feet and pulled her deeper into the apartment. His grip alone was bruising, but Ben kept fighting. Fear and adrenaline raced through her, making her blows to him so hard her hands burned with each hit.

"Well now, darlin'." His voice was deeper south than most of the locals. Her mind grabbed onto that fact as she kept fighting. "It's real nice to meet you, finally."

Ben lashed out, her knuckles making contact with his face. He swore and she tried to jerk away, but he grabbed her shoulder and held tight. He pulled back his arm and punched her in the face. Blood instantly spurted from her nose, making breathing harder and screaming impossible as blood poured down her throat.

As she fought for breath, he began to drag her toward her bedroom. She battled again, knowing if he got her to the bedroom, it would be another wall and door between her and help. She managed to trip him, but she fell too and he landed hard on her left leg. The screaming pain of the bone breaking make her vision blur.

"I love big titted women." The new vantage point allowed him to grab her breasts and rip her t-shirt from her body. The pain from her leg was too intense for her to even fight his grabbing hands right in front of her. "Kinda fat, though. Fucking lazy if you ask me, but it won't bother me."

He ripped her cotton pajama pants next, pulling them down to tangle around her knees. Her panties followed as his words became growls.

"No, no," Ben yelled, or at least tried to around the blood still flooding her mouth.

"Oh, hell, yes." He sat up to fumble with his belted jeans.

He was fat, not at all in shape, but he was too strong for Ben to fight. She'd taken self-defense classes, but she was at his mercy and they both knew it. A cellphone rang from one of his pockets, and Ben struggled again as he heaved himself on top of her and dug it out.

"What? Fuck." He scrambled off of her, slamming her head down twice onto the thinly carpeted floor, and then he was gone.

Ben turned onto her stomach and made herself crawl. He would be back. Over and over her mind screamed he'd be back to hurt her, so she ignored the pain radiating from everywhere and dragged herself to the door. She pulled herself up with the knob as the pounding on the door began.

"Ms. Riggs? Ben?" a young male voice called. "Hey, are you in there? I heard something."

"Thomas," she sobbed, trying to flip the locks with her blood soaked hands. "Get out of here. Call the sheriff."

"But--"

"Run, damn it," she screamed. "Get out of here!"

She heard him go, and finally Ben got the door open. She fell into the hallway to find Deputy Teddy Williams, Thomas and two other boys his age trying to get the keys from the manager.

"Help," she whispered as Teddy knelt beside her, pointing his gun toward the open doorway. "Get the kids out of here. Please."

She wasn't sure if he did, wasn't sure what was happening through the pain, but even that slipped from her mind as she passed out.

* * * *

"Okay, she's coming around. Ben Riggs?"

"Ouch," she mumbled as a gentle finger lifted her eyelid.

"Talk to me, Ms. Riggs. My name is Jarrod, I'm an EMT, and you were attacked. Anything in particular causing you pain right now?"

Ben tried to open her eyes but couldn't make them work.

"Your eyes are very swollen from a few hits you took to the face, but they're still there, no bone damage, luckily."

"Thomas and the other boys? They're not here?" She gagged on blood, and he tipped her sideways on a stretcher to spit it up.

"They're out on the sidewalk with Teddy and Sheriff Jefferson," he said. "Hand me more gauze, Mark."

"Mark?" She coughed hard and groaned when the pain spiked.

"I'm here, honey." Mark's answer was harsh and hard, but his familiar hand stroking her forearm was gentle. "I was finishing up at the nursing home when I saw the ambulance. We're going to get you to the ER, so just relax. You're safe."

"I don't feel good." She wished she could open her eyes and look at the EMT, but she held tightly to Mark's hand instead. "He left when Thomas and Davey and Sam knocked on the door. I told them to leave. I didn't want them to get hurt. Are they okay?"

"They're fine, sweetheart, I promise. They're just worried about you right now." Mark's soothing voice invited her to relax, but her adrenaline still poured.

"Ms. Riggs, can you tell me more about what happened?" Jarrod broke in. "So I can tell the ER what to expect. Were you raped?"

Tense silence surrounded her as she processed the question in her overwhelmed brain. He'd been on her, his pants had been open, and he'd touched her, but the phone call… Had it stopped him, or had she been in too much pain from her leg to remember?

Salty tears burned down her raw cheeks. The added pain surprised her heavy mind. She didn't think she could possibly handle any more. "I don't know."

"It's okay." Mark squeezed her hand again. "We'll find out for sure at the hospital. Don't worry for now. Jarrod, she's going out again. Go ahead, sweetie, don't fight it."

* * * *

From the sounds and smells, Ben recognized the hospital before she opened her eyes. Her face was intensely cold. When she turned her head, an ice pack fell to the side. Something tugged at the back of her hand when she reached for it, but she moved the coldness away anyway.

"Hey, Ben." She heard Mark's voice and opened her swollen eyes. He looked good, a little scruffy and worried, but good. "How are you feeling, honey?"

"Not…um…well." She reached her tongue out but found it was swollen and her lips were numb. "What happened?"

"Someone broke into your apartment through your bedroom window and attacked you. When Thomas and the other guys got to your place, you told them to run. I don't know if the attacker was still there at that point or not. You managed to get out, with a broken leg, and Teddy took care of things from there." Mark coughed, like his words were painful.

"It's fuzzy. Did he, um, did he rape me?" She whispered, because her throat hurt and she didn't really want to know the answer.

"The doctor doesn't think so, and if he did, then it was--how did he say it--superficial penetration. Like he didn't get to finish what he started, thank God." Mark held her hand when she tried to move it again. "You've got an IV in this one, sweetheart. What do you need?"

"I don't know."

"Then how about you go back to sleep?" Mark eased the ice packs back over her eyes, a soft towel covering her first. "You're going to feel like hell tomorrow, so you might as well sleep now."

"You're a doctor now too? Is there anything you don't do?"

"Not a doctor, not even an EMT. I just took the first aide class at the fire station, so Jarrod grabbed me when his partner was late," he answered, pulling the blanket over her arms. She had goose bumps she hadn't noticed until they were covered.

"You're really handy." Her mouth was sore and her tongue felt thick as she tried to stay focused and talk a little longer.

"I have my moments," he admitted. "But right now, you need to rest instead of listing all my amazing attributes."

She laughed, and it hurt her whole body.

"Damn, Ben, you need to sleep, right now," Mark ordered, and it didn't sound like a horrible idea.

"Okay." Before she even finished the word, she was pulled deeper into the black and fought for one more moment. "You'll stay?"

* * * *

"You bet I will. Don't worry about a thing." Mark watched her fall back asleep, her breathing and heart rate monitor showing signs of her tension easing. "I'm not going anywhere."

The bandages on her neck were bloody again, and rage bubble in him as it never had. He'd thought his sister was horrible for foisting her kids away like trash, he'd been angry after his father's senseless death, but none of that touched what he felt seeing Ben brutalized.

Some bastard had hurt her, had tried to rape her. If not for three teenagers dropping off homework for a friend in the apartment building, he would have succeeded. There was so much damage to her delicate body. She was tough, but the punishment was severe, and it did seem like a punishment to him.

The beating was personal, not random. Teddy himself had looked at her windows two days earlier, a vulnerable spot on the first floor. Upon checking them again after the assault they found a new, tiny hinge on the bedroom window that allowed the window to be opened differently, bypassing the lock.

The sheriff called in the detectives from Kansas City who handled the small town's major crimes. Flathead Falls just didn't have the manpower or facilities needed to correctly gather evidence to catch the bastard.

He and Ben had been walking around each other ever since she'd confessed her circumstances, and Mark had been okay with that. Hell, he'd been thrilled, because it was more than Ben had expected to give so soon. Here with him beside her bed, she still clung to his hand even in her sleep.

That didn't mean she wouldn't try to pull away once she had a chance to think about what had happened. He expected her to, but he'd already decided, while he'd been waiting for the doctor to finish his initial exam, he wouldn't let her push him away.

He liked her more than he'd ever liked a woman and he was edging into love. He knew it. A man like him would fall in love once, and he'd fall hard. His dad had made that prediction years ago. Ben touched something deep inside him, and he knew he couldn't let her get away.

Convincing Ben wasn't going to be easy, and he wasn't able to ignore the danger involved. She'd already had one attack, and the bastard could try to hurt his kids. Mark would get a security system for the house. He had a few more dogs at the second farm he could bring over until things were taken care of. He hoped those measures would be enough to quiet Ben's protests.

She wouldn't be the woman he was falling in love with if she didn't worry about their safety, but he wasn't going to let her be alone. Not when alone made her so damn vulnerable.

* * * *

Mark remembered the days when Teddy Williams was five and had run around naked, peeing on trees like a dog. It was hard to look at the man he'd grown into and take him seriously, but Mark was trying. With Ben sitting up only slightly, still barely awake, he wanted to tell Teddy to go have a sucker or something, but he was a deputy now and he was doing his best.

"Anything else, Ben?" Teddy asked solemnly.

"Just…red hair and big and…" She was breaking in and out of lucidity because of the pain medication, and while the police were trying to respect that, they needed to catch the bastard who'd hurt her.

"Stay with us a little longer, sweetheart." Mark rubbed her arms gently.

"He was familiar," she muttered. "From town, I'd seen him in a truck. Red hair, big belly, truck, southern…liked big titties."

Mark's hand froze and when he looked up, he could see Teddy's eyes had also gone sharp. Her description could have pertained to hundreds of men, but if he was a local that meant one person.

"You rest now, sweetheart."

Mark pointed for Teddy to meet him in the hall while Ben fell asleep again. He hated to leave her, but he wasn't going to talk in front of her in case the truth hurt more.

"That's Steven Redick," Mark said without preamble.

"He's been a person of interest," Teddy replied quickly. "The boys mentioned seeing the truck before entering the apartment building, and the sheriff immediately put out a watch for it. We've finally got a name on the woman too, a Ms. Victoria Bennet who goes by a dozen aliases. We're looking, Mark."

"Then why are you here?" he demanded.

"Because when we find them we have to have more than a hunch," Teddy explained. Though it made sense, Mark was still furious. "With Ben's description of the attack and everything else, now when we find him, we have a better shot at keeping him and Victoria locked up. There's been reports of them in Arkansas already."

"Then get the hell out of here and get looking," Mark snapped.

"Mark--" Teddy stopped and took a deep breath, and Mark kicked himself for overstepping.

"I apologize." Mark held both of his hands up. "Just... I know you and everyone else are doing your best, but Ben won't be safe until this is handled."

"There's a volunteer deputy on guard here, and we're not backing down security," Teddy said stiffly. "I'm heading back out, but my card is on the table, call if anything comes up."

"Okay. I will. And Teddy..." It was on the tip of his tongue to apologize again, but Mark couldn't do it. He just wasn't that sorry. "Find them."

Chapter 8

"No." Ben wobbled on her crutches but not on her reply. Mark hadn't expected her to back down, but that didn't mean he was going to give up. "How many times do I have to say it, Mark? I will be fine at my apartment, and I don't want to go home with you."

They'd been discussing it for over an hour. Ben was being released from the hospital, not because she was healed, but because her insurance was crap.

The three days allowed were up, and bruised, battered and broken, held together by plaster and string, she was headed home. If she'd quit being a mule, she'd just agree to come home with him and they'd both be better off. The woman was stubborn, but he didn't hate the trait. He figured she was the reason God had given him a pretty deep supply of patience.

"You would be fine in your apartment," he allowed. "You'll be better at the farm. I had a security system put in yesterday and brought over my dogs. The kids will just worry if you go back to your place, Ben. We'll all be over there all the damn time, and you know my place is bigger. How are the four of us going to move around your little apartment?"

"No, none of you are coming over." Her harsh tone reflected the pain Mark saw in her eyes. "No one. I'm going to put in my two weeks and get the hell away from all of you. I don't want you here. Why won't you understand that?"

It could have hurt his feelings, being told so point-blank he wasn't wanted, but he heard what she wasn't saying. She cared so much she would face her threats alone, rather than let them get hurt.

She tripped on her crutches, and he caught her before she went completely down, her body shaking with fatigue.

"Ben," he said softly, holding her. He was careful to give her plenty of leeway to escape if she needed to. After the attack, he didn't want her to feel trapped by him. "The nurse already went over all the instructions for what you need in the next few weeks, so I'll be able to take care of you. Let me help you."

"You could get hurt." Her voice was fierce, but she rested her face against his shirt in surrender.

"I could." He wouldn't lie to her. "But I'd rather help you fight than stand by and watch you get hurt or see you leave. I know you don't want a relationship, but you've got one. I wouldn't push like this so soon if I didn't care. I think we've got places to go and things to do together. I want years with you, honey, not days or weeks or months. Years."

"You don't know what you're saying," she whispered, stiffening in his arms. He thought she would push away and when she didn't he knew she was feeling much more than she probably wanted to.

"Yeah, I do. You just aren't ready to hear it yet, and that's okay." He kissed the top of her curly head. "I won't bring that up for now, but on the same note I can't just let you go. Not when I've got these plans in my head for us. If you're gone we won't have a chance to even try."

She was quiet, but she didn't pull away. He knew he'd hit something in the right area. Maybe she didn't love him right now, but she liked him and liked the kids and enjoyed the town and the people in it.

A plant couldn't be forced to sprout, but with the right kind of attention anything could thrive. The seeds had been planted in Ben, and they were already sprouting strongly in him. They would grow, he knew they would.

Ben was a woman made to love and give love; she just needed the right conditions and the right man. Mark was the man to make the conditions, the man to take in that love and shine it right back.

"What--what if it happens again?" He could barely hear the words she whispered against his chest.

"What if I get kicked by a cow tomorrow? It could happen. We'll try to prevent it. We'll do everything in our power to keep you safe, but we'll deal with the blows as they come. Don't worry about tomorrow. It'll bring its own troubles."

"That's from the book of Mark, isn't it?" she asked, the familiar Bible verse bringing a smile to her face.

"Yep, one of my favorites. Trust me, sweetheart, and you know what? If that's hard at this point, then trust God. He doesn't always work in mysterious ways. Sometimes He works very predictably through people who care about you."

"I know you're right, but I'm terrified. Sometimes it consumes me to the point I can't even move. I hate being this afraid, but I can't shake it. This mess won't go away, and I can't fix it."

"I know, baby." He strived to find the right words to comfort as he carefully hugged her closer. "And no one's faulting you for being afraid. But be scared where I can keep an eye out for you until all this blows over. It can't last forever, sweetheart, and when it's done we'll be ready to see where we can go."

"You think you might love me?" The pain medications were loosening up her tongue.

"Yeah, I really do think that's where this is going. I can see you and me loving each other until we're brushing each other's dentures and counting warts on the dogs."

"I hate warty dogs," she mumbled, and then the quiet stretched and he waited. "I'm ready to go home now, Mark."

"With me?"

"Yes. With you."

                              * * * *

The nurse gave her one more shot before she left, so Ben knew she was pretty out of it when they got to the farm. She'd stopped by once briefly to drop off Kira, but hadn't gone inside the house.

There seemed to be two styles of farm families, she mused as she looked around. One style was farmhouse chic and spotlessly tidy. Then there were houses like Mark's. It was cluttered, and dust bunnies congregated in the corners. The rugs had been shaken out recently, but had probably never been washed. The vacuum cleaner stood in the mudroom and had a nearly full canister from what Ben could see.

They probably cleaned when they couldn't avoid it any longer. She'd bet they did the dishes when they were out of spoons and butter knives, because it was hard to spread peanut butter with a fork, though they might try.

It was a home, and it was where Mark was welcoming her. The kids at the kitchen table were willing to help too. It was the most wonderful place she'd ever been.

"Hey, Ben." Kira's boisterous personality seemed muted, and while it was a relief, Ben wished circumstances were different so she could have a big hug. She could use one. "Are ya hungry? We were going to make some soup and PB and J."

"I'm not right now, but thank you." She leaned on Mark as he helped her release her crutch foot from the metal strip at the door frame.

"I think I'm going to help her lie down for a while, squirt," he told his niece. "I'll get her settled, and then we'll head out and do chores. How's that sound?"

"Okay, I guess." Kira pouted a little, and Ben knew she wanted to help.

"Maybe you could read to me later? You said you were reading *Stuart Little* last week, and it's my favorite."

"I can do that." She perked up. "And if you're hungry when you wake up, Thomas can make you some more soup. We've got tons in the cupboard, because Uncle Mark just went shopping at the super store. There's ice cream too, if you want."

"Sounds great." Ben smiled, though it pulled incredibly on her broken face.

"Come on, honey." Mark helped her across the kitchen to one of the four doors. "You'll be in my room. It's right off the kitchen, so we'll be able to hear you if you need anything."

"But--"

"Hush, Ben, you know I don't mind you using my room. I'll bunk with Thomas, no problem."

"Yeah, Ms. Riggs," Thomas added. "No problem. I'd let you have my room but it's at the top of the stairs, and your cast would probably make that hard."

"And my room is at the middle of the stairs so that wouldn't work either. And I don't have a door."

"No door?"

Mark answered, "It's a jog in the floor plan. The room works great for now, but one of these days it'll need a door. Come on, let's get you laid down."

"I'll share, though, when you don't need your crutches so much anymore. Uncle Mark's kind of a slob," Kira called as they headed into the room.

"Eat your dinner." Mark shot his niece dirty look Ben recognized as fake, especially when Kira giggled.

Like Kira warned, Mark's room was indeed a mess. A pile of dirty laundry occupied a corner, clean clothes were folded haphazardly but on the long dresser, not in the drawers. It smelled like a man's room, not gross though, just manly.

His deodorant still hung slightly in the air, a really good smell that made Ben think instantly of him and she liked it. The bed was wrinkly, but she could see the sheets were fresh if not ironed and the blankets were the homemade kind. The old quilts were tossed on and smoothed by arms too small to reach the middle.

"Kira," he said with a smile. "She tries to change us boys, says we're too messy and don't think about stuff, but she's only a step up from us.

She tries though, and her room is probably the cleanest of the whole place outside of the milk room. We would have made the place presentable if we'd had more time. Sorry--"

"Don't be." She eased to a sitting position on the edge of the bed. "It's a farm. You work hard, and there are more important things than ironing sheets. I like your house, Mark. It's a home."

"It sure is." Working together, they got her onto the bed and he put a pillow behind her head and another under her broken leg. "And we're happy to have you here. I left a walkie-talkie for you. It's one of Thomas's from when he was a kid, but they've got fresh batteries and good range."

"You are such a thoughtful man." The meds were dragging her down with every moment she was on her back surrounded by his scent. "I think I'll like being in love with you. You won't mind not having more babies?"

"I've done it twice, honey. Of course I'd love to have more if you want to adopt, but I'm also happy to share Thomas and Kira with you. I could definitely use a partner who has your wonderful way of dealing with the monsters." He tucked a curl out of her eyes as she smiled a little at his words.

"They're nice monsters."

"Yeah, they sure are. I'll bring you some cool packs for your eyes. You just rest. Need anything else before I go?"

"A blanket?"

* * * *

Mark returned her goofy smile. It was at least partly drug induced, but he didn't care. "Of course you can have a blanket. This one's my favorites. Mom made it for me when I was a kid."

He pulled his covers over her body, careful to make a tent over her leg and swollen toes. She'd be sore, but for now she would sleep and heal. Even though the situation was an ugly one and the circumstances were harsh, it was still amazing to see Ben lying between his sheets. Content in seeing her there, Mark just sat and stared for a long moment, watching her breathe.

It would be all right with him if she spent the rest of her nights right where she was. Soon he hoped he'd be welcome beside her.

A woman in his bed was a novelty. He hadn't had one there since Thomas came to live with him fulltime. There'd never been a woman in the past he'd been willing to endure the kids' questions for. Ben was different. She was changing things, changing him. He said a little prayer that she would heal quickly and then left her to sleep.

The kids had a bowl of soup and a peanut butter and jelly sandwich waiting for him on the counter when he entered the kitchen. It wasn't the supper of champions, but the soup had vegetables in it and he'd bought wheat bread so it wasn't a total loss either.

He took a bite of his sandwich and turned to them. They both looked concerned. There wasn't much more he could do to reassure them though.

As he chewed, Mark grabbed two little ice packs from the freezer. They were covered with princesses and were the ones he used in Kira's lunch bags. He grabbed a towel and then snuck back into his room. Ben only moved slightly when he put the ice packs in place and since he wanted her to sleep, he didn't engage her more than he had to. He left her resting and headed back to the kitchen.

"So is Ben moving in, like, permanently?" Kira asked after he closed his door. She scowled at her brother who must have kicked her under the table. "What? You said if I wanted to know, I had to ask. So I did. You're a butt, Thomas."

"Enough kicking and name calling. And yes, Kira, for now Ben's going to stay here." Despite Ben's drugged admissions Mark hesitated to make any announcements on the timeline, especially to Kira. "You guys know all the rules to help keep everyone safe, right? You both know how to arm the security system? Even when we're all home, I want it on."

"Yep, and we can't tell the passwords to anyone," Kira added. "Not even Missy Ann and Lena. Not even to Melody, Thomas."

"I know," Thomas growled at his sister, his new girlfriend a popular point for teasing now, especially when Kira thought he was spending too much time with the older girl instead of playing with her. The dynamics were changing as they got older, but every new stage was one Mark enjoyed.

"Okay." Mark nodded, slurping the rest of his soup straight from the bowl. "I love you guys, and I can't let anything happen to either of you."

"Not that Kim or Pierre would care," Thomas muttered.

That was truer than Mark would ever admit to either of the kids, especially with Kira still wanting contact and change with her parents. "I would care, Thomas. The diapers and puking are finally over and you two are getting pretty fun to be around. If anything bugs you or anyone approaches you, run like hell. Scream bloody murder, and if you're wrong we'll apologize later. I'd rather have you overreact a hundred times and have to apologize than have you hesitate even for a moment. Kira, are you coming with me to do chores?"

"Yep." She wiped her face on the bottom edge of her t-shirt. "I love you too, and I'm good at screaming. Don't worry."

"Good." He kissed her head when she hugged him tight around his waist. "Thomas, can you stay in with Ben? I gave her the radio, but she's pretty out of it."

"Yeah, no problem. I'll work on my chem lab." The teenager ambled over to grab his full backpack off its peg, on the way bumping shoulders with Mark. "I don't like all the new rules, but I'll be careful. I'll keep an extra eye on the brat and on Ms. Riggs at school too."

"I know you will." Mark squeezed his nephew's shoulder. Hugs still happened on occasion but more and more the shoulder pats and handshakes were becoming more appropriate. It was a transition Mark had made with his own father in his teens, but there were times he missed the hugs. "Use the radio if you need anything while I'm out."

"Will do," he replied, and plopped back into the kitchen chair, ready to work. "Have fun with the cows."

"I always do."

Chapter 9

Ben wondered how far she would have to push before Mark's patience wore out. She sat at her desk, her foot on a stool, and blew out a breath. Mark hadn't wanted to drop her off at school, but when she'd insisted, he'd relented. He'd also kissed her before she left the car. It had been sweet, barely on the mouth with just a little nibble of tongue, and she'd really, really been a fan.

It had been over seven months since she'd been kissed, and Mr. Mark Dougstat did not disappoint. She was a sexual woman, and even though Mark was big and strong and had a nice body, she hadn't been sure if they would sizzle. He was a good man, so if there hadn't been fireworks, she would have been happy to put effort into firing up a little chemistry between them.

She shivered at the memory of his kiss alone, the spark far more potent than 'little'.

Patient and a good kisser. She was toast.

That wasn't the tragedy it could have been. The police were sure they would catch Victoria and her accomplice. Victoria, such a pretty name for such a crazy person. Ben shifted, uncomfortable as flashes of the attack ran through her mind. She shook her head, not willing to indulge those thoughts. The attack had been too bold and too much evidence had been left. The police would catch them both and then she and Mark could have peace.

"Ms. Riggs?"

Ben looked up from the test she should have been grading. She'd zoned out again, something she'd been doing on and off all day when not actively teaching. The kids were being easy on her, and while she knew that wouldn't last, she appreciated the reprieve.

Melody Ramsey, Thomas's girlfriend waited at the end of her table with a stack of notes. She had a sympathetic look on her earnest, round face. She wasn't the prettiest girl in school, but she was certainly one of the sweetest. Ben was glad Thomas had seen beyond the baby fat and bottle cap glasses when he'd looked for a special girl to spend time with.

"Thanks, Melody. Do you need a pass?"

"Nope, I'm on secretary duty," she answered. "Oh, and Mr. Dougstat called like four times just to check on you. Mrs. Murphy said to tell you until you're officially engaged he needs to keep the calls to twice a day."

Ben laughed. "I'll tell him she said so. Thanks."

Her room was quiet, the kids at a school-wide assembly the principal had excused her from. It was no wonder she'd zoned again. Exhaustion crept in and she wanted her pills, but until the school day ended, she'd have to make do. The notes from Mark were an unexpected bright moment, and she laughed as she flipped through them.

She picked up her phone after reading Mark's second message, the same as the first; *Just Checking* and called his cellphone. He'd made her memorize the number the night before. It hadn't been hard with her steel-trap mind for numbers, but she'd let him drill her on it for an hour while they cuddled on the couch during a movie after the kids were in bed.

"Hello." Mark's brisk tone was his normal greeting, never looking at the caller ID on his phone before answering.

"Hey, farmer man." She winced at the tired, scratchy quality of her voice.

"Ms. Riggs." His tone instantly warmed.

A smile emerged between yawns at his quick change. She loved how she affected him. "Mrs. Murphy says you can't call so much."

"She told me I can have two calls a day until we are engaged, then it turns to three a day until we're actually married. It goes back to two a day until you're pregnant, after which I'm clear for every hour," he replied, and she could nearly feel his amusement across the line.

"That's nice she has a system down." Her heart clenched at the reality of never having Mrs. Murphy's permission for hourly calls. The unexpected jolt hurt, and her pain must have shown in her voice.

"Ben…" His hesitance made it clear he knew what was on her mind.

"So, did you call for a specific reason, or just being nosey?" She couldn't talk about babies and that stuff, not now.

"Mostly nosey," he admitted, allowing the change, but she knew his patience was matched with persistence. If he wanted to expand on the baby conversation one day, he would. "But I wanted to let you know, I'll be there at three-thirty after I pick up Kira. Does that work for you?"

"It does. You can drop me off at my apartment, so I can grab some more clothes and pick up my car."

He was quiet on the other end, and Ben waited without comment. It was a pretty fair compromise, she thought. She wasn't trying to leave his house, but she was asking for more than he'd ideally like to allow.

He had to remember she was a grownup; a hurt, troubled one, but still a capable adult. Since she was feeling a little better, she needed to remind him.

"Okay, no problem. We'll stop by your place for clothes and your car. I was going to offer to change your oil anyway. How about we get your stuff and have some dinner? Thomas can run over after practice and drive my car home while I check yours out."

"Yeah, that would work." She hadn't thought about the possibility of her car being a danger. She'd never forgive herself if someone got hurt because of her, and though the police had been watching the apartments and her car was in the garage, she'd learned there were no guarantees with safety. "You know, maybe I'll just grab some clothes and leave the car."

Silence met her reply, and she thought for sure Mark would jump at winning his way. "No, I can look it over and make sure it's safe. It'll be better for you to have your transportation available when your leg heals. Even if you can't drive it while you're in your cast, it'll be safer locked in my shed than in town."

"I don't like that it's just there waiting for her or someone to tamper with it. Maybe we should have Teddy help too."

She could almost hear him nodding over the phone. "Sure, he can help me change the oil while we're under it checking the brakes and everything."

"Thanks for the offer on the change but it doesn't need oil. I had a full tune-up before I drove south."

"That was smart."

"Yeah, don't let all the schooling fool you, I've got a little sense," she teased, because thoughts of cut brake lines and people intentionally trying to hurt her and others made her ill and she couldn't take any more negativity. She'd devoted too much time to it already. "I'll wait by the office doors for you at three-thirty."

"Sounds good. I'll see you in forty minutes."

"Forty minutes it is. Goodbye, Mark. Drive safe."

"I will. See you soon."

She thought he might say more, and waited, but instead he hung up and that was okay too.

Good to his word, Mark arrived at three-thirty on the dot. Kira waved wildly from the backseat of the older model Buick. He jumped out of the car and gave Ben a peck on the cheek before taking her backpack and purse.

"Thanks." The gentleman treatment and attention made her feel a little shy. She'd been thinking about him all day and seeing him face-to-face again, more handsome than her imagination gave justice for, made her want to blush and giggle.

"You're welcome. Did you have a good day? Pain okay?"

"I did have a good day. We had a quiz and started the second half of our chapter," she explained. "I feel pretty rough, but I'm okay enough."

"We'll get you fed, then back to the farm to put your leg up with a few ice packs."

Mark helped her with her crutches and cast, and she eased down into the car. "You're such a nice man."

"For you, I'll be the nicest man you've ever known," he promised quietly, and brushed another kiss to her cheek. "Buckle up, sweetheart."

"Hi, Ben," Kira said from the backseat though she didn't look up from the worksheet she was working on.

"Hi, Kira."

Mark shifted back into drive and checked all his mirrors for kids still milling about after school. "We'll finish things up quickly so you're back in time for your next pills. By then I know you'll want those ice packs."

"That sounds amazing," she admitted.

"Far from amazing, honey, but we'll do the best we can to help you feel better."

Amused and feeling really warm and special all of a sudden, Ben enjoyed the quiet for two minutes. Then she listened with a half ear as Kira detailed her entire day from debating what to wear, to which questions she'd answered in class and how she'd known the answers. She ended with the number of cookies she'd snagged from her friend's lunch box because Mark had forgotten to pack her some.

When the pizza arrived at the apartment, Kira finally stopped talking, but only because she was half-starved and had her mouth full. Thomas barely nodded at Ben when he arrived, and like his sister, dove into the food. The siblings headed out in Mark's car as soon the meal was finished . It was for the best they not be near her vehicle.

Teddy Williams's deputy car pulled into the driveway as Ben and Mark made their way to the shared garage behind the building. One of them had a lock, so the manager had given her that one. They were also replacing all the windows and doors in her apartment so she could return. If she ever did.

"Hey, Teddy." Ben was tired and worried, but she smiled for him. He was a good man and was doing a big job in confronting Victoria on her behalf.

"Evening Ben, Mark. How are you two tonight?"

Mark stayed beside her as she navigated her way to the garage in the grass. The gravel path he walked on fouled up her crutches and made it impossible to stay upright. He kept a hand on her elbow. It didn't help much, but it was nice to have it there. The grip tightened a little in Teddy's presence, and she couldn't imagine why.

"Doing well tonight, Deputy." Mark's stiff, formal answer confused her more. She couldn't see any reason why Mark wouldn't like Teddy. "Ben wants her car, so I'm going to give it a thorough going over before we take it out to the farm."

Teddy nodded and removed the aviator style sunglasses he wore nearly constantly. "Not a bad idea. I just took a class for vehicle tampering in KC. Can I offer some help?"

An hour later, Ben sat at the side of the dingy garage on an old five-gallon paint can and watched Teddy and Mark shifting around under the car. Teddy had rigged a mirror tool to see underneath and when nothing showed, they'd laid in the dirt to check everything else.

"No, damn it, boy, what did they teach you in class?"

She bit back a giggle at Mark's exasperated tone when Teddy once again pointed out a wire. The young deputy's intentions were good, but from what she was hearing he wasn't knowledgeable enough about automobiles to be much help.

"Son, that's the brake line, intact and complete. We do not want to monkey with that." Mark's instruction was back to patient, and though Teddy's reply was muffled she was sure she heard some stammers.

The difference fifteen years could make, she thought. Teddy was a fine young man, sweet, kind and strong. But Mark was also all those things, along with having life experience and seasoning. The trials of his life had left him a little gruff at times, but always willing to find joy and help others. Teddy would get there one day.

When both men pushed out from under the car, grease and grime clung to their faces and clothes. Guilt bubbled, but she pushed it down. They'd offered, and she had to accept help to keep everyone safer.

She plastered a smile on her face. "So?"

Mark grabbed a roll of paper towels the apartment manager had left in the garage and tore off a bunch, rubbing at the grease on his hands. "Looks good. Nothing out of the ordinary. Right, super cop?"

Teddy's face turned so bright red she could see it even in the dim light. "Yeah. Looks good."

"That mirror thing you made was a really good idea," she said.

Mark wasn't being mean and his light teasing wouldn't hurt Teddy, but she still wanted to prop him up a bit.

"Yeah," Mark instantly agreed much to her growing pride in the man she cared about. "It took a load off my mind knowing there wasn't anything hanging down here. I bet Jack Jensen down at the auto shop would give you a quick lesson on the basics, so you can tell the difference in brake lines and trip wires."

Teddy coughed a little and stood to his full height, two inches taller than Mark. "I think I'll do that. I spent a week in the darn class, I'd like for it to be more useful than knowing how to duct tape a hand mirror to a hockey stick."

"That was smart, though." Mark tossed his paper towels away and held his palm out to her. "Keys, please."

She dug in her bag and found them. Her heart pounded at the thought of Mark driving her car if anything was wrong. For all they knew, Victoria could be a master mechanic and top bomb maker. She could have hidden something tiny in there that looked like another part of the engine.

"Ben."

She looked up and realized Teddy had moved toward the front of the garage, and Mark was closer than before.

He put his hands on her shoulders, and she forced herself not to jump. "Honey, it's fine. I'm just going to take it for a spin around the block. Teddy is going to give me a police escort. It's not every day a guy gets that offer without the cuffs."

Dropping the keys into his hand was one of the hardest things she'd ever done. He grinned and his confidence did what it always did, gave her courage and reminded her to trust him.

"Now, no burn outs." She pushed for a scolding tone and he smiled.

"I'll bring her back in one piece."

Fifteen minutes later they were on their way home. Back to the *farm*, Ben instantly corrected herself. The farm was not yet her home. It certainly had everything she wanted in a home--space to roam, people to love, kids to keep her young, animals to tend and spoil, and a man who could also fit that role.

Thomas had called Mark's cell and asked him to get more milk and cereal. Ben laughed as he ran in the store and picked up two gallons of milk and four boxes of breakfast food.

"I'll say it again," she said when he tossed the bags in the backseat, "I know teens eat a lot, but I don't know where he puts it all."

"I don't know either, but I remember those days and always being hungry. It didn't matter what was available, if it was food and it wasn't rotten I wanted to eat it." Mark laughed. "Mom said in the span of a summer our grocery bill doubled just to keep up with me. Milk, cereal, vegetables, yogurt, beef, chicken, soup, hell, it didn't matter. If she had it in the house, I'd eat it."

"And now the tables have turned. It's good you're taking care of the kids. Your mom is probably still tired from keeping you from eating the furniture."

"Yeah." He tensed at the mention of his parents, just like he always did, and her teasing fell flat.

Silence stretched between them. She hadn't asked Don questions when she'd thought things bothered him. If the situation was one she could help with in any way, she always knew he would come to her when he was ready. With business deals and issues, she'd never expected to be a confidant, but she'd been a willing ear when Don decided he needed one, which hadn't been often. With Mark things had to be different.

"Mark, when did your dad die?" She asked the question gently and hoped the time was right.

"Ah, about a month before Kira was born," he answered.

"Was he sick?"

"No. He was out plowing. We'd had a fight about timing on the field. I wanted to wait a week. He wanted it done right then, so while I was out with some friends he went out to plow. A storm hit and his tractor tipped on him."

"Oh, Mark, I'm so sorry." His words were blunt and didn't invite more questions. She could feel the loss and grief, as if they were tangible things in the car, even though a full decade had passed since the incident. "I'm so sorry for your loss."

"Thanks." He didn't rebuff her hand when she reached across the bench seat and put hers on the one he had resting between them. "It's been a long time, but Mom never got over him dying. They'd been married too long, so she needed a new place. I took the kids in after she moved."

"I'm glad that worked out so well." Ben understood the pain of losing parents, and she was glad Mark hadn't lost both entirely.

"It did. I'm glad she's happy. She's in a retirement community. Last year they went to Ireland for a week," he replied.

"You miss her?"

"Sometimes. Thomas does too. She and Dad raised him the first few years, but he understands now how sick she was after Dad died."

"Kids know."

He nodded. "Your parents died when you were a kid."

"Yes, but it was different, I think. They died in a car accident. I was seven, so I remember being horribly sad and shaken, but my aunt took me in right away. I think it would be harder for Thomas and Kira to have their parents alive and uninterested. I hate that my parents died, but I know they didn't have a choice."

"Right, I think that little thing with their parents is either going to put them off having families of their own one day, or it'll have them making me a grandpa before I'm ready." Mark's grin held a note of sheepishness. "There's a therapist I talk to once in a while, and she says the same thing."

"You'd be a wonderful grandpa." Ben smiled at the thought of him rolling around with babies and taking the little ones out to pet the calves. "They're both smart though, so I bet you're not too worried."

"Not so much. They are good kids."

"And you've got no problem stepping in and making sure they don't get in over their heads too early."

"I already had the sex talk with Thomas, and Kira still thinks boys are disgusting. I think I have some time." He laughed, but she heard the strain in it. "Dear Lord, I hope I have some time."

They pulled up next to the garage. Thomas and Kira were getting out of Mark's car, milkshakes in their hands, which explained the time difference.

Even from a distance, Ben could hear them throwing insults at each other.

"Uncle Mark! Thomas called me a booger eater!" Kira shouted.

"If the shoe fits, then I call it a booger eater." Thomas walked behind his sister, flipping Kira's ball cap off her head.

"Shut up. I do not eat boogers. You eat boogers." She chased after him and smacked his back with her hat. "And I'm telling Melody too. I bet she won't want to kiss a snot licker!"

"Like I said…" Mark laughed as he helped Ben out of the car. "I think I've got time."

Chapter 10

"Ben, can you get that?"

She looked up from the paperwork her insurance company had sent about getting approved for counseling. The phone was a long way away, but Mark was farther or he wouldn't ask. She maneuvered her crutch and winced when her broken leg hung funny at first. She'd never broken a bone before, so it was all new and incredibly painful.

The yellowed phone buzzed shrilly as she made her way across the tile. Being tired from working all day and being dragged down by the constant ache was making the relatively simple task harder than it needed to be. What she wanted to do was go to bed.

"Hello, Dougstat residence."

"So you are staying out there."

The lack of greeting might have startled Ben if she hadn't recognized the speaker. There was no mistaking her aunt's voice.

"Hi, Aunt Willy." Ben tried for a peppy, upbeat tone. It didn't work, but she tried. "How's Seattle?"

"Fine. It's raining again. Now, why in the world are you at the Dougstat farm? You've only been back in Flathead Falls for a few months, and you're barely out of your widow garb. What are you thinking shacking up with some man? I raised you better than that."

"Aunt Willy, who told you I was shacking up here?" Ben reached with her crutch to pull a chair closer. The cord was long enough for her to walk to the table to sit, but she didn't want to move that far.

"Mary Johnson and Bernice Finkle both called me with the news," Willy huffed. "Unacceptable, young lady, especially for a teacher. You've got an example to set for your students, and living under the same roof with an unmarried man and his bastard children--"

"Kira and Thomas are not bastards," Ben snapped, increasingly tired and frustrated with her aunt's incessant rant. "They are Mark's niece and nephew, and he is their guardian. He's a wonderful man, and he has graciously offered to help me right now out of good Christian duty. You should know about that, Lord knows you told me every day about doing your duty."

There was a gasp on the other end of the line and Ben wished back her words. Fighting with her aunt never went well. Ben always lost. Always.

"Well, if he's doing all those wonderful things, you just scoot out of there, missy. A little broken leg won't kill you, and Mary said the new windows were put on your apartment days ago," Willy said coolly. "Playing the damsel in distress doesn't suit a woman of your size or years, Bennie. Have some pride."

"We'll see, Aunt Willy."

"We'll see? See what? He's a farmer. I raised you to do better for yourself. You should consider moving to a bigger city."

"I'm happy here," Ben insisted.

"I'll even pay." Willy's gallant offer caught Ben's attention. Her aunt was frugal to a fault. "Yes, I will. If you gain entrance to an acceptable school to finish your degree, I will foot the bill for the move and medical school."

"Medical school?" Ben hadn't thought about going into the medical field in years.

"Yes. Something with a specialty, cardiology or neurology I'm thinking would be best. In another six years you would be Doctor Benfri Riggs Wiggert. It has a nice ring to it." Her aunt sounded uncharacteristically pleased, and part of Ben hated to burst her bubble. A bigger part of her wanted to lie down and not have to talk to her again until the idea of doctorates was out of her old head.

"Aunt Willy--"

"Think about it," Willy broke in. "I trust you will make the right decision. Shacking up with some man, being a glorified nanny and milkmaid, is not who I raised you to be. I'll look around and start getting you some applications."

"Okay, Aunt Willy, you do that." The nanny and milkmaid comment made Ben want to fire back with something ugly and harsh. But to fight would have meant prolonging the conversation, and that was the last thing she wanted to do.

Kira slid across the vinyl beside her on fuzzy socks, a happy grin on her face. She opened her mouth to say something, saw the phone and did the locking motion over her lips. Ben smiled and she didn't think after her aunt's tirade she'd be able to do that anytime soon.

"You'll see," Willy said, a long drawn out sigh punctuating the warning.

All Ben saw was Kira reaching down to the kitchen floor and attempting a handstand. The kid was too darn funny.

"I know what I'm talking about," Willy continued. "After your parents died you needed a firm hand to bring you out of the disrespectful, self-destructive path you were on. I may be older, but I'm willing to be the one to put your head on straight again."

Kira plopped on her butt and looked up, her big green eyes trusting and full of good humor. Ben's eyes burned with the need to cry, but she refused the tears life. Her discomfort must have shown though, because Kira hopped to her feet, crossed the distance between them, and gently wrapped her thin arms around Ben's shoulders.

Aunt Willy was wrong, very wrong. It shouldn't have come as a surprise, but Ben had always looked to her aunt for the advice that mattered in her life. She was the one who'd raised her and loved her in a way. But it wasn't going to be her way, Ben decided as she wrapped her free arm around Kira.

"I'll talk to you soon, Aunt Willy."

"You'll get out of that house then?" Willy asked in satisfaction.

"Nope, not for a while," she answered, content with her answer.

"Ben--"

"No, don't worry about me, Aunt Willy. I'm in a good place and will think very intently about the things you've said," Ben interrupted, tugging Kira's fire-red ponytail.

"Of course, I'll worry," Willy bristled. "You're my only kin, and I love you. Even when you make your horrible decisions. Just don't shame me, Benfri."

"I love you too, Aunt Willy."

Ben placed the receiver back in its cradle and leaned on one crutch as she brought Kira in closer. She smelled like a kid--dirt, sweat and sunshine, the best things in the world.

"Did you talk to your aunt?"

"I sure did."

The little girl looked like she wasn't sure what to make of her answer and really, Ben didn't need her to understand, just needed her to keep being sweet and young for as long as possible.

"How about we watch a movie?" Ben asked, the aches of the day real, but she wanted to listen to Kira talk nonsense and nine-year-old business.

"With popcorn?"

"Okay, why not?"

* * * *

Mark didn't hate Teddy. That would have been like hating puppies and vanilla ice cream. No one hated those things, not seriously anyway. But the younger man's presence grated on his nerves. He was a good deputy, and was doing the best he could on the case considering he wasn't a detective. The kid hadn't done anything wrong.

What Mark couldn't handle was seeing Teddy's face light up whenever he saw Ben. He and the deputy were going to have to have a talk soon. Ben was closer in age to Teddy, but that didn't matter, because what was growing between Mark and Ben had only gotten stronger since she moved in.

Teddy moving in on his territory wasn't what Mark worried about, not really. Ben was faithful and true. He just didn't want Teddy to embarrass himself or put Ben in an awkward place.

Usually Saturdays were a reprieve from the overeager pup, but this time he'd brought a therapist for Ben to talk with about the attack. The woman was one of Teddy's many cousins, and that had been a positive sign for Ben. She'd been having some rough dreams, and Mark could understand why. That level of personal danger weighed on a person. She did well a good eighty percent of the time, but the other twenty, got very long.

Since he was spending his nights on the couch, only feet from his room, he could hear when she woke, gasping. She didn't scream or cry out, but her panic induced breathing woke him from a dead sleep every time.

He would have rather been in the house, sitting at the table with her in case she needed him. Instead he was out cleaning the chicken coop, trying to pass the time until he could make sure Ben was all right.

"Oh, hey there, Mark."

He froze. How the hell had Teddy snuck up on him? He turned and didn't even try for a smile. The grin on Teddy's face faltered, and Mark figured every drop of his displeasure showed.

"Sorry to interrupt." Teddy's nerves filled the tiny chicken coop. "I just left Karin with Ben. They were going to have some coffee, and Karin told me to get lost. Do you need any help?"

Mark looked Teddy over. He wore jeans and a collared shirt. His shoes were the kind Thomas liked, kinda wimpy looking with accent stripes on the sides. He looked like a young twenty-something who did well for himself. Which he was, Mark reminded himself. Other than knowing so little about car maintenance, Teddy was a resourceful guy. Who had once peed on his truck tire.

"Doesn't look like you're dressed to be helping on a farm, Teddy." Mark tossed the last of the straw into the far corner as the chickens pecked closer to see the new presence in their home.

"I brought rubbers."

They looked at each other a moment, Mark letting Teddy's words sink into the younger man's head. When they did, Teddy's ears lit fire engine red.

"I mean, shoe covers," he stuttered. "I help my granddad sometimes, and I keep a pair in my car."

"Yeah, I know what you meant." Mark decided since the subject was practically up, that he'd use the opportunity to talk with Teddy about Ben. "Which reminds me... You understand why Ben's here, right?"

"Of--of course." He was tripping over his words like a teen in interrogation. "You've got a good setup, and it's great you're helping her while her leg is hurt."

Mark nodded. "You're right, it is good and I'd help anyone I could. But how many people have you known me to welcome into my home, Teddy? Ben's special to me."

The red was ebbing a little, but transferred to Teddy's cheeks as he understood better.

Mark nodded as he thought Teddy was starting to get it. "Yes. She is very special, and Teddy, you're a really nice kid, but if you're entertaining--"

"Wait a second," Teddy broke in. He cleared his throat as he pulled himself up to stand taller. "Okay, I'll be honest here, Mark. Ben Riggs is a hell of a lady. If things were a little different, yeah I would have asked her out already. But things aren't different. The second I found out you were in the picture, I threw in the towel."

Mark stared at Teddy a second and then laughed. "Why the hell would you do that? I'm not saying to start fighting now, but a few months ago there was no reason not to."

Mark liked the grin that came to Teddy's face and he hoped he found someone nice soon. A nice kid like him deserved a good girl to come home to. Just not Ben.

"You might be old and have shit on your shoes most of the time, but everyone around here knows what a good guy you are, Mark. And the more I learned about Ben, the more I knew you were what was best for her. She's just a friend now. It hasn't been my intention to step on your toes, but I'm not going to stop caring for my friend because it makes you growl a little."

"Damn, boy." Mark shook his head, feeling his forty years in seeing little Teddy Williams stand up to him. "Where the heck was I when you grew up so well?"

Teddy grinned. "Probably out milking a cow or pitching shit."

"Probably." Mark set aside his pitchfork. "Well, I've got a spare set of coveralls in the other barn. If you've got the rubbers and the time, I've got some sheep pens I was going to get mucked out today."

"Karin said to be gone for two hours. I'll grab my boots."

Three hours later with no Ben or Karin in sight to stop them, they'd gotten the whole barn mucked out and bedded with fresh straw. Mark and Teddy leaned against their pitchforks, sweaty and dirty.

From his place, Mark could see Ben and Karin exit the side door of the house. Teddy had said something about a text message a few minutes earlier, but wasn't making any rush to get out of the borrowed clothes. He was breathing a little heavy, not used to the hard work, and while it amused Mark, he didn't rub it in. Not after getting more work done in a morning than he'd planned for the whole day.

"Wow." Ben looked between his and Teddy's shoulders into the barn. "You two got a lot done out here."

"Yeah, he's a pretty rough taskmaster," Teddy said. "No wonder Thomas is so tough on the football field. This farm work isn't for sissies."

"Darn right," Ben agreed, and though she laughed, Mark could see the vestiges of tears in the red rims of her eyes and swollen nose.

When she looked at him though, her eyes were clear and genuinely smiling. He breathed a sigh of relief he hadn't realized he was holding. Whatever had happened had helped. Karin had made a friend for life in him.

"So." Karin's voice was as tiny as her stature. "Are you giving me a ride home, Teddy, or do you have to go pull calves or something?"

"No calves to pull 'til spring." Mark was fighting himself not to go to Ben and wrap her up in his arms, but everyone was staying light so he tried as well. "But I'll be sure to give you a call, Teddy."

"Yeah, and I'll call you next time Mrs. Kennedy's cat gets stuck in the runoff drains," Teddy replied with a chuckle. He shrugged out of the borrowed clothes and Mark accepted them.

"I wouldn't mind helping out Flathead Falls's finest," Mark said.

Ten minutes later the Williams cousins were gone, a clean barn and hopefully a more clear-headed Ben left in their wake. Mark scrubbed up in the laundry room and listened to Ben working in the kitchen. He had another half hour before he had to pick up the kids from raking leaves at church. He hoped it was enough time to feel out the status of Ben's situation.

"It was good," she called when he turned off the water.

He looked over his shoulder and found the doorway empty. "What's that, honey?"

"The meeting with Karin. Before you asked, I wanted to let you know it went really well. We talked, she gave me some great resources, and we're going to meet again if I want."

He dried his hands and walked into the kitchen where she was washing coffee cups. There was tension knotting her shoulders, and he realized she expected him to grill her about everything. It had been his plan, but he quickly reevaluated.

"Good, I'm glad it went well." The space between them was too much. Part of him thought she might need it, but another part didn't care. He closed the distance and tucked his chin on her shoulder. "She seemed nice."

"Oh, she is." Ben's assurance was immediate, and she relaxed under his touch. "I just don't really want to talk about it anymore."

"I suppose," he said slowly, "it would be like beating a subject to death."

"Exactly." She relaxed deeper into his embrace, drawing his arms around her middle. "Did you know it's okay if I stop thinking about it all the time?"

He frowned a little, not sure what she needed to hear from him. "What do you mean, baby?"

"I mean, it's okay if I enjoy my life while I deal with this other garbage," she explained. "Karin said I'm getting mixed up because I've got some really wonderful and exciting things happening, while I'm trying to recover from some ugly things. It's okay if I don't let the business with Don and Victoria and now the...attack consume me."

"That makes sense to me."

"Yeah." She blew out a breath and turned until they were nose to nose. "It makes sense for me too. I thought there was something wrong with me because I wasn't-- I don't know how to explain it."

"You were worried you were dealing too well. Other than the night stuff, you've been doing great. I suppose you were concerned you were in denial or something."

"Exactly." Her relief filled the room. "I was worried I was bottling a problem for later, but I'm not. I'm just...I'm dealing with the issues at hand, but I'm happy too. It's been a while since I was genuinely happy. I guess I didn't recognize the feeling."

"Well, that's a relief."

She gave him a confused look at his exaggerated sigh.

"It is," he insisted. "It's good to know you aren't a head case."

She burst out laughing. "And were you worried I was?"

He brushed a kiss to her smiling lips. "Naw. You've got a good head on your shoulders. And you're smart enough to know when to ask for help."

"I am smart enough to ask for help," she agreed and brushed her lips back to his. "And you're sweet enough to make sure I get it. Thanks for being so wonderful, Mark."

"That's not something you ever have to thank me for."

"Sure it is. How are you feeling after cleaning the whole barn?" she asked.

"I'm fine. Might be a little sore later, but for now I'm okay. Teddy will feel it tomorrow, I'm sure."

"Probably not." The teasing was back and he could smile for real because she did. "Karin mentioned he does lots of weight lifting. He's scrawny but tough."

"Okay, rub it in already that I'm an old guy," he said sourly.

"My old guy." She pressed her lips gently to his.

It was one of her first shows of uninitiated affection. She never pulled away or discouraged him, but always in the past had let the first move for closeness be his. He'd been waiting for her to be comfortable enough to take the first step and it thrilled him.

"My mature, sweet, patient, wonderful man. Thanks for being all those things."

He kissed her back, keeping the tone light and sweet. "If we're going to make this work, then I want to be everything you need me to be. Even wonderful on occasion."

"Just on occasion?"

"It's the times between those occasions that will make the wonderful all that much better."

"Okay, farm boy. I'll take occasionally."

Chapter 11

Victoria was angry, and angry never went well for the people around her. She looked at the latest batch of pictures on her digital camera and fought the urge to throw it across the room.

Bennie was fine. A little battered and bruised but nothing lasting. If Steven would've finished the job, she could move on and head for Nevada like she'd planned. But no, he'd screwed it all up because he'd acted like a little scaredy bitch in the face of some stupid kids.

For the past week they'd been hiding in plain sight, and it grated on her. There was no reason they shouldn't have been gone. Well she gone, Steven dead, and the delay infuriated her.

She clicked the button for the next picture and Ben's broken face made her smile a little. It wasn't enough though. If she wanted anything done right, she had to do it herself.

But nothing short of killing Bennie herself had seemed as scarring as rape. If she'd had a pet, Victoria would have taken joy in gutting it while it screamed and adorning Ben's apartment or, even better, her school classroom with its dead body. But no such luck. Ben hadn't even gotten a fish since moving to Missouri.

There were so many options and facets of torture Victoria could have employed, but nothing had played out as sweetly as physical force in an intimate act. Don had told her Bennie was a virgin on their wedding night. A sweet little, untouched flower and if things had gone right, Steven would've destroyed her.

Now, Victoria had cleanup to do, and she despised cleaning up after other people.

"Come on, Victoria," Steven snapped.

She rolled her eyes. The scenario they'd practiced before he'd attacked Benny had gone to his head, and suddenly he thought he was in charge. Moron.

"But we can't leave yet." Victoria stuck out her lip in a tiny pout. "One little thing, Steven, and you didn't get it done. I love that you broke her leg and made her look so ugly, but you didn't do what I asked."

"I know what you asked. I started, I hurt her good, but I couldn't be caught." He eased into a fatherly, patronizing tone that grated on her nerves. "They might have tracked you from me, and I couldn't let that happen."

They wouldn't have found her, no way. Cops were dumb, sheriffs were worse, and Steven would've held out just long enough for her escape.

"How about this, sugar tits." Steven leaned in close with his beefy hands on either arm of her chair, caging her in. "She's staying at my friend Mark's place. It's on our way south. We'll stop by for one final 'goodbye' before we disappear. How's that sound?"

"That," Victoria said, her mind suddenly teaming with ideas, "sounds promising. Do you still have the car equipment?"

"It's already packed if you'd scoot your sweet ass." He indulgently tweaked her nose, and she was too busy thinking to get pissed. "Now get your shit together. We gotta move."

Chapter 12

"No offense, really Mark, but chickens don't like me," Ben insisted, hobbling behind him on her walking cast. It was the weekend after Thanksgiving, nearly a month since the incident and she hadn't gone home yet.

She could have, probably should have, but she'd let Mark talk her into staying until her cast came off. She knew he was gearing up for his next argument when it came off in two weeks, but she couldn't justify staying any longer.

Victoria hadn't made any contact, hadn't called or sent anything, so Ben agreed with the sheriff to back down surveillance in small doses. They were staying vigilant, but the immediate threat level had decreased. They believed Victoria had had her fun and moved on before getting caught. Ben wasn't so sure, and Mark always armed the security system, so she knew she wasn't the only one who felt like the next shoe could drop at any minute.

"Oh, damn! Those things are on my car!"

"Like they're going to hurt it." Mark laughed when she pointed to the chickens swarming her unused car.

No one had driven it since they'd brought it to the farm, no need. Though it was her left leg that was broken and she *could* drive, it proved more tedious than practical. So her car just sat there, adorned with a flock of disgusting chickens and their poop.

"What's your thing with birds, honey?" he asked as he filled a pail with corn. "There's no reason to be afraid of them. Especially chickens. If they're bad natured you just catch 'em, cook 'em and show 'em what part is the nugget."

"I don't know. They creep me out. All birds, I hate them all. Did you ever see the Hitchcock movie about them?" She shivered at the thought.

Stephanie Beck

"Oh, please." He chuckled, and she didn't find his amusement at all funny. "Honey, it's just a movie about a few crows, not a big deal. Birds might poop on you, but chances are, they won't hurt you."

When two hens moved closer she squeezed behind Mark like the five and a half foot sissy she was. "I don't care if they're fluffy marshmallows on the inside. Make them go away, please. I'll do anything."

"Ah ha, the promise I've been waiting for." He turned and wrapped an arm around her middle, thick with one of his sweatshirts. "Sending me into battle, milady? What does your brave knight get?"

"A kick in the pants if that one touches me," she whimpered as a black rooster closed in for the corn.

"You just keep a proper reward in mind for later." He laughed again and gently nudged the rooster in another direction. "I trust you to deal fairly with me."

Ben stepped behind the swinging half-door of the granary when he let her loose. She watched as Mark, her hero, rounded up the chickens. It wasn't hard; the things were evil but they were dumb to boot, so they followed the corn. The dozen on the hood of her car didn't seem to want to move though, jumping and fluttering around as if they expected it to heat up for them like Mark's usually did.

He whistled, shook the pail, and swore at the birds with no effect. The two border collies he'd brought from his other farm looked on with no interest, and finally he headed toward her.

He was shaking his head in disbelief, but he didn't look aggravated. It took a lot more than some stubborn chickens to faze him. She smiled when he grabbed fishing net from the granary wall and gave her a tiny peck on her cheek. His ingenuity never failed to amuse and amaze her.

Mark made it three steps when one of the birds jumped onto another on the car. Stupid birds, she thought, she'd have to scrub her hood with bleach to get it clean.

They were fighting with each other, and Ben was about to yell at them when the hood erupted in flames, shaking the ground and toasting the chickens. She watched in horror as Mark jumped out of the range of the explosion.

"Mark!" she screamed and fought the door's latch to get to him.

"Call the fire department," he shouted. She thought he looked unhurt as he ran to get a hose.

Ben pulled her cellphone from her coat pocket and made the call, staring at the carnage in front of her. Chickens, those pitiful chickens, were running around with their feathers on fire, screaming in pain and terror. The car continued to actively burn. Ben couldn't make herself look away.

The chickens were suffering, but there was nothing they could do. Mark brought the hose, but it wasn't enough so he also used a shovel to put out the little fires that sparked and burned.

When screaming, burning chickens neared her, Ben looked away. She didn't like birds, but would never wish such a painful demise on them. Nor would she wish the grim chore of putting them out of their misery on Mark. Thank God the kids were gone, she thought, both at friends' houses in town, far away from this latest catastrophe.

In amazing time, the fire department arrived with two trucks. They hooked into the well and soaked down not only the car but the surrounding buildings that were beginning to smolder. Mark was a volunteer firefighter, but he let the dozen men do their jobs as he stood beside her.

When the fire was out and the car was deemed safe, the sheriff stepped in. The men looked at the car, Ben staying back in the granary at Mark's request. It had to be tampered with. When he looked to her, his earnest face tight with fury, she knew she was right. Victoria hadn't forgotten her.

* * * *

"Honey, you can't know that for certain." Hours had passed and Mark and Ben were finally back in the house sitting at the kitchen table with security armed. Mark was trying to reassure her, but Ben didn't want to hear it. "No one knows how long the bomb was sitting in that car before it blew. Teddy was saying they've got a lead on a couple who match Victoria and Steven's description in Tennessee. They're probably miles from here."

"Does it matter if it was a month ago or two days ago?" Ben demanded. "She wants me dead. Even if she is in another state, she can come back. What if Thomas had taken my car or you decided to move it? Or hell, what if Kira decided to play near it?"

"You just said 'what if' three times. 'What if' didn't happen. Everyone is okay, and except for the car itself and a few chickens there is no permanent damage. Take that for what it is and be grateful. If you spend your time with what could have happened, if I spend time going over it like that, we'll just make ourselves sick."

"But Mark--"

"No." His fierce denial made her jump. "No 'but Mark' for this, because you and I both know the most likely scenario. You would have gotten into your car, alone. You would have burned to death like those damn chickens. Then what? Thomas and Kira are looking at you like you're the best damn thing to ever come into their lives, and Ben, what would I do? What the hell would I do without you, loving you the way I do?"

There were tears in his eyes despite the anger in his words, and those tears hit Ben like a fist to the gut. He loved her. He'd known her three months and he did, he really did.

She was devastated at the thought of him being hurt. She remembered that moment when she'd thought he was in danger from the car and she shook. Her throat was too tight to force words from. Without him, so much changed. Everything that mattered in her world changed if he wasn't in it.

He stood and walked to the sink, leaving her alone at the table. The tension in his shoulders, in his whole body, screamed to her. Abandoning her chair, she wrapped her arms around his back. He turned and hugged her tight. Her healing ribs ached, but she didn't mind. She finally understood what he meant. The initial inklings of love hadn't been obvious, because there hadn't been the bursting sort of moment she'd expected.

She loved him. There was more to learn about him, but there was no doubt in her mind he was hers. Life without Mark--calm, steady, messy, farm-smelling Mark--would be unbearable.

"You're everything." She choked on tears as he pressed kisses to her temples. "I-- Mark, I don't have the words."

"I know how you feel about that." What could have been a try for a chuckle was forced from his throat, but there was no humor there, only emotion. "Everything I want to say is stuck in my head, but it never seems like enough. No words are enough for what you are to me."

"I love you." She gripped the fabric of his shirt tightly in her fingers. "It hurts how much I love you right now."

"I never want you to hurt, baby," he whispered, easing his hold on her though she didn't want him to.

"I think it's a good hurt." She leaned back only enough to press her mouth to his. "I want this over. I want this woman gone so I can have you, Mark, so I can be part of your family."

"I'm not going to let her stop us," he promised between nipping kisses all over her mouth. "I refuse to let her take this away from us. Tell me you feel the same, Ben. Tell me I matter enough to take the chance."

"You do, and that's why I don't want to take the chances." Tears leaked down her cheeks, but he kissed them away. "If something happens, and today showed it can--"

"Today showed that God's on our side." Mark shook his head even as he continued to press kisses to her eyes. "With Him on our side, who can be against us?"

"Lots of people can. Look around, Mark. Even if Victoria wasn't breathing down my neck, there are other things that keep popping up. My aunt, Steven, and who knows what your family will think when they hear what's happened since you met me. God is great, you'll never hear me say anything different, but common sense is important too," she replied. Mark was sweet, he was smart, but she couldn't just let go of all of the things that kept happening around them.

"Okay, you're right. Things haven't gone as smoothly as either of us would have liked since you came back, and I wish like hell I could change that. So are we supposed to just crawl under rocks, Ben? Because let me tell you right now, if you decide to do that, I'm just going to move my rock closer to yours. We can choose to live in constant fear apart and fighting each other, or you can trust yourself and Flathead Falls and me to do everything possible to keep everyone safe. There's opposition, you're right, but we've got a lot on our side too. Big things on our side."

She sighed at the words. He was always right, even when the situation wasn't. "How do you come up with the words that actually make me want to change my mind? It's not fair--none of this is. It's not like I want to leave. I just know I should so you'll be safe."

"We're safe, honey. You stay with us, stay with me. I don't think I can handle you leaving me, Ben, not forever," he admitted. "Not even short term until this gets figured out. You're shaking so badly. You need to lie down."

"Will you come with me?" Ben pressed her cheek to his chest for the comfort his heartbeat offered. "Just to lay with me for a while?"

"No funny business?" His humor was a sign he was easing back a little on the intensity of the moment, just like she needed for the shaking to stop.

"You'll be safe with me," she promised. "Scout's honor."

"Okay, honey," he said, brushing more kisses to her hair. "I gotta say holding you sounds like the best thing in the whole world right now."

"Then come on." She broke his hug and tugged him along with her. She didn't know when she'd be all right with not having her hands on him, making sure he was really okay, but it wasn't going to be anytime soon.

* * * *

The kids found them an hour later, asleep in Mark's bed under a single light cover. The adults were both fully dressed and curled together like two giant kittens. They'd heard about the fire from Thomas's friend's dad who was a sheriff's deputy, and had hurried home not sure what to expect.

There'd been nothing to see outside except Ben's car was missing and there were a few scorch marks on the shed. The security system had been armed, and Thomas had meticulously reset it upon entry.

Neither of them looked hurt. Tyler's dad had assured him no one had been, but seeing them safe and sound was a huge relief.

"I think we get to keep her, Thomas," Kira whispered, looking into the bedroom beside him. "I talked to her and she said they were working on grownup stuff, and Uncle Mark pretty much said the same thing when she first got here. I just wonder how long it's going to take them to stop talking and, you know, be together."

"Do you want that?" Thomas wanted his uncle to be happy, but never at the expense of his sister.

"Oh yeah. She's nice, and she knows about girl stuff. And I think she loves Uncle Mark. Since Uncle Mark is kind of our dad, Ben could be like a mom."

"We have a mom and dad." Just the thought of their crappy, absentee parents made Thomas scowl.

"Yeah, but not really," she answered. "Sara's mom said Uncle Mark was better than a lot of dads and we're freaking lucky to have him."

"Sara's mom has to quit cussing so much," Thomas muttered.

"But you know what I mean. We're a family now, but I think we'd be even better with Ben. She knows how to iron my shirts." Kira's tone was wistful, and Thomas realized she'd been missing having a mom more than he thought. Big brother responsibility made him want to give her all he could. He hoped Mark didn't screw it up.

"I think he loves her," Thomas added, tugging his sister from the door. "I guess we'll just have to wait and see what happens."

"Should we wake them up?" she asked, reluctant to be pulled away, but Thomas kept on. Part of Mark not screwing up was going to be letting them have some alone time. Kira wouldn't understand yet.

"No. Let's get supper started."

Kira's disappointed expression instantly brightened. She spun toward the cabinet and started searching. "Oh, good thinking. We'll pull an 'Uncle Mark'. We'll feed them, and then grill them for details. What's a good soup for getting people to spill all the important details?"

Indulging his sister was easy, and in this case it gave Uncle Mark a few more minutes alone with Ben. "What are our choices?"

Chapter 13

Back at work with more grading, Ben wanted to scream. Piles upon piles of homework surrounded her with no end in sight. The semester was coming to a close, and she had to finish her grades by break to get report cards out on time. At least it was normal, and that was a very good thing for her sanity.

She'd opened up her inbox for late work and the kids jumped on it at the last possible moment. That meant she had four days worth of work to finish in two. She was actually contemplating asking Mark to help, but she wasn't sure that he would.

Over the five weeks she'd lived at his house, she couldn't help noticing he didn't help the kids with their homework unless they asked him questions. He didn't look over Kira's work, didn't read to her at night either, which had bothered Ben until she realized Kira read to Mark every night out of one of her juvenile novels.

The paperwork he kept was computerized. His notes online were particular and short, nothing detailed, but his mind was a steel trap. The man forgot nothing and even on bigger shopping trips never made lists though Ben needed one to run little errands.

Ben frowned, trying to place what really bothered her. The kids in class were studying, so she rummaged through her drawer. She found the welcome card under her planner and looked at it carefully. Mark's name was typed. She tried to match the scribbles around the note to his name, but none did.

She thought of the menus he didn't read, the manuals he never opened, and the church newsletters that went untouched. She'd overlooked them in their context, but maybe there was something more to the situation.

It finally came to her as she stared at the friendly little card. There was a reason behind all of Mark's idiosyncrasies, and he hadn't told her. She wondered if he even knew.

The day finally ended and just like always Mark waited outside the principal's office with Kira in the car. She was talking a mile a minute before Ben even sat and she didn't get the chance to talk to Mark about what she suspected.

When they got home he headed for his woodworking shop with Thomas at his heels. They were making Christmas presents for Thomas's friends and Mark's associates.

Ben fed Kira dinner and helped the little girl get the soap out of her hair during her shower. After a few stories, she tucked Kira into bed. The days were much shorter, and Kira was one of those kids who woke up ready to go, ran hard all day, and then crashed by eight o'clock. It was a beautiful trait.

Ben armed the alarm system and hurried out to the two car garage only a step from the house. Mark used the heated space as his workshop. Thomas was in the corner of the kerosene-heated building with his iPod togs in his ears, painting yet another birdhouse.

"Hi, handsome." Ben watched a bead of sweat roll from Mark's scalp, caught it with her finger, and wiped it on her jeans. "How's it going out here?"

"Good," he replied, dropping a kiss on her cheek. "We've got these to finish for the orders at church, then we only have the mini ones to do for gift baskets. It seems like we get a few more orders every year."

"Very nice. You and Thomas are incredibly talented." The workshop was messy, but filled with the clean scent of wood and sawdust even the kerosene couldn't cover. Like everything in Mark's work life, there was a quiet efficiency tempered with plenty of dust bunnies and a trash can that needed to be emptied.

"How's the grading?" he asked, interrupting her musing.

"I'm half-done. Just when I think I'm making progress, I swear the stuff on the bottom reproduces. I'll work on it for another hour tonight, and I think I'll be able to finish tomorrow."

"Barring any more paperwork fornication." His smile lifted the heaviness weighing on her heart about his secret.

"On second thought, maybe I'd better get up when you do."

"Yeah, that might give you a little more time. It seems like everything is cutting too close." He moved onto the next set with the smooth efficiency she admired. "Your cast comes off tomorrow too."

"How could I forget? I can't wait." Her leg was well healed according to her doctor, and she dreamed of being completely brace free. "So I thought of something today."

"Imagine that," he teased.

"Something I hadn't expected," she continued. "It was kind of a surprise, but all the clues were right there the whole time."

Mark froze and shot his oblivious nephew a look, but Thomas didn't see it, too busy with his music and project. "Oh yeah?"

"Yes." She hesitated, but there wasn't a gentle way to ease into the question and there was no better time. "Mark, have you ever been tested for dyslexia or any other learning disabilities?"

The clamp in his hand fell, the metal ringing sharply on the concrete floor. He didn't look at her, just bent over and fixed the clamp, moving on to the third before he answered, "No. I don't have any problems. I don't like reading or writing, but I'm not stupid."

"Of course you aren't stupid," Ben gasped. "I would never ever say anything like that, but I was just thinking today--"

"Maybe don't let your thoughts run that way again," he suggested, moving onto the fourth birdhouse.

"Mark, I'm allowed to think whatever I want. I just asked because I'm a teacher and it's my job to notice things like this," she said stiffly. "I would never do anything to hurt you."

"Well, don't worry about this. I'm not broken. I don't need Super Teacher to fix me." He finished the birdhouse and wiped glue from his hands onto his jeans. "I'm going to check the cows. I don't want to talk about this again."

He left, not storming out or causing a scene, but not turning back when she called his name either. She'd never imagined such a heated response. Very little bothered him and in the last two weeks since the car fire they'd gotten so close, easily telling each other everything they could think of.

He'd shared with her so much more about his childhood and the trials of raising two kids. The alcoholism he continued to fight and beat every day had come up on several occasions, and he'd been open and honest about it. The dyslexia could be an embarrassing thing in some situations, but he had to know she would never put him down.

"His dad used to call him stupid."

She looked over to find Thomas painting with ear phones still in.

"All the time. He'd say my mom got all the brains and it was too bad there was nothing left for Mark."

"That's horrible," Ben said, shocked.

"Yeah. He used to say the only thing Uncle Mark could be was a farmer, and used to stand over him at the kitchen table while he struggled to read. Mark was good at memorizing the lessons, so he'd stay up all night with Grandma to avoid getting beat," Thomas continued. "Uncle Mark had me and Kira tested really young. I couldn't figure out why until Grandma told me."

"Poor Mark. You know it doesn't matter to me, right?"

"Yeah, I mean as long as you don't try to fix him like he said. He's got his own way of doing things, and it works for him. He doesn't want to learn any other way, so if you try to push him…"

"After what his father did he would probably hate me," she finished. "I won't. There's no reason to change if he's content. I just want him to be happy."

"I know." Thomas's smile was much older than his sixteen years. "It's a pretty tough spot, not just because of Grandpa. My father tried to talk my mother out of signing custody of us over to Uncle Mark because of the dyslexia. He called Uncle Mark a moron and all that crap like Grandpa did. We almost ended up in a boarding school in Sweden because of it."

"Well, heck, isn't your dad a scientist? He should know better." Disbelief and disgust at the behavior of Mark's sister and her husband just continued to grow.

"Yeah, you'd think. He's an ass. All his associates call him a donkey, even if he's a brilliant one. Perfection is such a big thing for them, and Mark didn't fit the mold then, and he still doesn't."

Ben heard the bitterness in Thomas's voice. Mark wasn't the only one Thomas's parents had rejected. She couldn't imagine what the young man felt, knowing in the eyes of his mother and father he wasn't worth the time and effort to raise. It was something no child should have to know, but he did. Kira did too, or would very soon.

Mark's influence shone through in Thomas though. He was disappointed and hurt, but Thomas was also steady and disciplined. When Kira worked through her parent issues, Ben didn't doubt Thomas would be a guiding light.

"Your uncle loves you so much, Thomas," she told him, because even though she knew both the kids realized their positions in Mark's heart, it never hurt to remind them. "And you are special to me. Between school and home, I've seen all your wonderful qualities, and you should be proud."

"Yeah, I know. I love him too. He's just taken a lot of crap for not reading right. From Grandpa and from Pierre, but Uncle Mark never quit. He fought for us. But the dyslexia, it's not an easy thing for him to talk about."

"Okay. I understand. Thanks for explaining it. How often do you listen in when we think you're listening to music anyway?"

"Not often. Old people are basically boring." Thomas shrugged and went back to painting.

Despite the heaviness of the topic, Ben left the garage with a smile. She wanted to chase after Mark, but she wasn't going to leave the kids alone, not with Victoria's threat still lingering in her mind. Mark would be back after he'd had some space. She took out her paperwork again and with newfound vigor, plowed through the papers.

When she was down to less than an inch of papers she eased back and enjoyed her cooling cocoa. The semester was nearly over and she'd survived. Now all she had to do was worry about Christmas. There were only a few gifts for her to wrap, but as soon as her papers were turned in, she'd have the time.

Stomping boots broke Ben out of her thoughts. It was after ten and Thomas had ambled through earlier and grabbed half a package of string cheese before going to bed. The house was quiet and cool, and Ben hoped Mark was ready to mimic it.

"Hey, handsome." She gave him space when, like usual, he went to the sink first to wash his hands and get a glass of water.

"Hi." He didn't look at her.

Since her arrival a few things had changed in the house. The dishes were done more often and laundry was folded when it came out of the dryer, but the house was still very much the home Mark, Thomas and Kira had lived in for years. It just smelled a little better, and there were fresh cupcakes more often.

"How are the cows?" Ben asked, setting aside her pen and putting the papers in her backpack.

"Still mooing." He dried off his hands and arms with the fresh kitchen towel. "About earlier, Ben... I was an ass. You didn't deserve that, but I don't want to discuss my problem. I'll discuss anything else with you but this--"

"I understand." She jumped to assure him, though he still looked doubtful. "Mark, I do. The only reason I even thought of it was because I was thinking how odd it was that you help in all these areas of your life, yet you aren't the head of anything. You don't run for county office or for the farmers association though I know you've been asked. I'll just say this and then we can let the issue die, okay? Can I say one thing?"

"Okay." He braced himself, and it hurt her heart to see him so defensive.

"If the reason you've never done those things is because you have a hard time reading and writing, I would be more than happy to read and write papers for you. I'd do anything to help, and we would never talk about why between us, we just wouldn't," she promised.

Mark turned away from her and carefully threaded the kitchen towel on the oven door handle. The whole situation embarrassed him, and because it killed her to see him so uncomfortable, she hurried to finish what needed to be said so they could move on.

"Dyslexia does not mean stupid. It doesn't. Your dad was from a different time. He probably didn't realize, but we know now it's a brain thing that doesn't connect with intelligence. You're a smart, thoughtful man. That's all we'll say about it, if that's what you want."

"That damn boy." Mark finally turned to her and shook his head. "I should have known he would listen and know things I'd rather he didn't. You're right about Dad. Please don't think badly of him. In his way, he was trying to help. I've made this work, but if that other stuff comes up, I'll let you know."

"Good. Then we can let this die."

"Thanks, Ben." The softness in his eyes and the love he showed through them made her melt. "And I'm sorry again about earlier. You are a great teacher, and I'm grateful you'd want to help. I love you."

"Well, you've never once made me feel bad for any of my problems, and I'm not about to do that to you." Walking was much easier with her brace, so crossing the distance between them took no time. "I love you too much to ever try to hurt you."

His smile turned just the slightest bit wicked, and she wondered for the millionth time what Mark Dougstat was going to be like when she got him into bed and not just for a nap. They'd cuddled and crashed a few times when the kids were at sleepovers, but other than that they'd kept things relatively innocent. Ben loved to snuggle and make out with Mark, but it was taking its toll on her.

Mark tugged her close, easing back to a minor recline against the counter so she could lean into his body, putting them hip to hip and chest to chest. His hands settled at her lower waist, just above the swell of her butt, and they would stay there too, maybe massaging a little, rubbing her sweetly.

His fingers spread and she held back a sigh, not at the monotony, because the way he made her feel was nowhere near redundant, but because she knew she'd go to bed unsatisfied.

"What's wrong, baby?" He stopped in his ear nuzzling at her sigh. "You forgive me, right?"

She nosed his cheek until his lips were closer to hers. "Of course I do. That's not it." She pressed on until he was fully engaged in the kiss.

He kissed like the thorough man he was, taking the time to rub lips first to get them tingling before slipping in his tongue. Never with too much force at first, not choking, just enough to ignite her fire like a good boy scout. He fanned the flames, rubbed her lower back.

Being snuggled to him so intimately made her want to move closer, but that was torture in itself. His semi-constant erection was another tease, a delicious one she wanted and wasn't getting.

She pulled back. She never did that, but he let her, looking at her with confusion. "You don't forgive me, Ben?"

"I already did," she snapped a little and stepped out of the embrace to shake herself. "It's just...this is driving me crazy, Mark. All the kissing and touching and teasing is putting me on edge."

"It's just a little sparkin' darlin'." His good ole' boy drawl didn't help. "If you don't like it..."

"I love it," she moaned. "But because of my leg I can't get into the shower to take care of things afterward, and I can't in bed because Kira sometimes visits me. I'm going a little bit nuts, so just give me a second."

The confusion cleared up, and his gaze turned from a little wicked to absolutely naughty. "You're saying you're hot and bothered and not able to take the edge off? That's the problem?"

"That's about it. It's been almost a year since I've had sex, and before Don turned out to be an ass we had an active, satisfying sex life. The teasing on top of the abstinence is making me a little edgy."

"I see."

"I don't think you do," she told him bluntly. "I'm talking multiples. Nightly. It was great, and I want it with you, because you are so incredible. We are going to be great together, but I know you, Mark--you're going to want to wait until we're married, and when my skin isn't burning just to be touched, I want that too."

"So you want me to back off with the kissing and fun?" He slowly closed the distance she'd put between them as if a "yes" to that question might not mean a whole hell of a lot.

"Yes and no. I know if I say 'yes' and you back off, I'll just want you all the time and think about what I'm missing. If I say 'no' then I'm going to just have to deal with this frustration," she wailed. "It sucks!"

"Come here, honey." Mark drew her back to her semi-prone position over his body. "I think I can help with this problem of yours. I can't have you uncomfortable, and I honestly didn't even think about you not being able to blow off steam. I'm probably going to go blind within another week or two at the rate I've been going."

"Just think of all those poor murdered kittens. That's something my aunt used to mutter about that sort of thing. 'Every time one of you kids succumbs to temptation, Satan kills a kitten.'"

"That's horrible." He chuckled and slid his knee between her legs, pulling her tight against him. "I know you'll worry about the kids in about two minutes but don't. Kira's out for the night, and Thomas is too. Just let me do this for you, okay?"

"Do you really think you can get me off through my clothes in the kitchen?" she asked in disbelief.

"Oh, ye of little faith," he all but growled.

"Okay, I take that back," Ben said quickly as his mouth latched over her nightshirt and instantly soaked the fabric covering her nipple. "Mark!"

He attacked her nipples, adoring them with licks and kisses and driving her wild with little nibbles as well. The hard leg that was cuddled to her sex began to move with firm strokes against her clit.

Her pajama pants offered minimal resistance to his ministration, and Ben didn't hesitate in grinding back. She moved with his rhythm and bit her lip to keep from yelling out. Every little thing he did made her aches worse instead of better.

Desperation spiked. The thought she might not be able to finish and all the foreplay would go to waste swept over her. But Mark held her hips firm when she started to rock harder and faster.

"I can do this all night, sweetheart," he assured her, moving one hand from her hips to squeeze her nipple between two fingers. "No reason to rush, just relax and let it all come together. I bet you're soaking my jeans, aren't you? I'll never wash them again."

His voice, his pinching fingers, the firm grasp on her ass, and his hard leg that just wouldn't quit had her so close she had no response. He caught her involuntary whimper with a hard kiss.

Ben was branded by his kiss, so much more potent than their previous ones. It held something more, and that more made Ben's legs twitch helplessly. Mark didn't try to slow her, only dug his fingers harder into her ass and kissed her deeper, taking in the strangled cries of her climax.

He eased back with his leg as she began to come down. She tried to catch her breath, but between the orgasm and the shock of just how good and wicked Mark was she knew it might take a little time.

* * * *

Mark should have known making Ben feel good would make him feel like the biggest guy in the world. Her limp, sated body against his had pushed him from his constant semi-hard on to full on attention, but she didn't seem to mind so he didn't pull his pelvis from her soft stomach.

She was so soft and sweet; he couldn't imagine how she would taste in other areas, because if he did he would embarrass himself. Probably by moaning or crying or coming in his pants like a teenager. He breathed in the sweet scent of her hair instead.

"How was that, sweetheart?" He tried not to grin like a fool when she only moaned.

"That worked," she finally mumbled, not making any motion to move away from him.

"Not so bad for both fully dressed in the kitchen, huh?"

"We're going to catch the house on fire when we're actually horizontal and naked." She sounded a little awed, but mostly exhausted.

"Absolutely," he agreed. "But you're right about waiting until after I've got my ring on you to invest in bedroom fire extinguishers. That doesn't mean I'm not always at your service, little lady. We aren't married yet, but you're still my woman, and I'm going to take care of you in every way you'll let me."

"What about me taking care of you?" she asked. "Wasn't the added burden one of the reasons you didn't like the other women in your life?"

"You take care of me just fine, Ben, better than fine." He looked her up and down, the satisfaction on her beautiful face more than enough to inspire him later. "And about reciprocation... Like you mentioned, I've got the option to go blind. As long as you don't mind keeping Kira busy while I'm in the shower, I've got that covered. Nothing distracts a man like a little girl yelling in to ask if he's done yet."

"Okay." She relented for the time being but couldn't put the issue away. "But for how long?"

"Well." He hadn't been sure on the timing, so he'd been treading water a bit. But since she'd brought it up and seemed willing to talk about the future, there was no time like the present. "I got you a Christmas present yesterday."

"You didn't have to. You better not have spent much on me or I won't be happy."

"Yes, you will," he promised. "I think you'd better let me give it to you early."

* * * *

"What does my Christmas gift have to do with us screwing?" Her question was naughtier than he expected. The light flush along his cheekbones was usually an indicator of his surprise. She was having a hard time curbing her words, though, the pleasure making her feel loose for the first time in too long. "Er, did you buy me a vibrator or something?"

"Good night." The curse was colored with embarrassment. "Hell, no."

"Oh, buck up, big boy," she teased. "Grownups can have toys too."

"Yeah, but that's a little personal. If you want one of those I'll let you pick it out."

His stilted assurance told her it would take a lot of work to convince him of the value of toys in life. It would be a fun tutorial when the time was right.

"No, what I got you is right, here--one second, right here." He reached up onto the top shelf of cabinets and pulled out a red gift-wrapped box.

The box in his hand was a small cube. She started hyperventilating.

"Whoa, honey, relax." He pushed her into a kitchen chair as she tried to catch her breath. "Hell, I knew it was too soon. Forget it for now, okay?"

"No." She grabbed the hand that held the little box before he could put it back. "No, Mark, not too soon. Just surprising. There is no way in hell I'd forget a red jeweler's box. Can I still have it?"

"I, ah, I guess." He sat in the adjacent chair as she carefully tore the thick paper. "It's not exactly what I wanted to give you. My parents' rings have been in the family for years, but I can't ask Mom to part with hers."

"Of course not." She pried the little box open to find a modest white diamond on a thick gold band. The simple beauty wasn't lost on her, and it reminded her of the man who had chosen it. "Oh, Mark."

"I know it's not big or all that great, but it comes with a big promise." He knelt in front of her, and her heart hammered against her chest. "A life with you is something I've thought and prayed about, and I've known for a while you're the only woman for me. I'll always be a farmer, God willing. Crap will always be on my shoes, and my job won't end at five o'clock. That said, I'll also work every day I'm able to make sure you have the things you need and maybe even a few you want. I'll take off my shoes before coming into the kitchen and during those long hours away, I'll be wishing I was back with you. Will you marry me, Ben?"

Ben laughed through her tears during his proposal. She'd made too many mistakes to deserve a man like Mark. She was still paying for too many of them to ask him to share her burdens, but it didn't matter. Those missteps didn't even touch the amount of love she had for him. She would pay her debts with or without Mark. She'd rather persevere and work through them all with him than any other way.

"I-- Mark, that was beautiful." She wiped away an errant tear before kissing his upturned mouth.

"Answer me, woman." His tone was gruff, though she could tell he tried to make it playful. She saw he really didn't know her answer and considering how hot and cold she'd blown in the past months she could understand.

She took the ring out of the box and pushed it onto her finger, the sizing just right, and she held it to her chest above her heart. "I would be the happiest woman in the world to marry you, Mark. I--after everything I've said--thank you for asking. I don't deserve it, but thank you."

He shot to his feet, taking her in his arms with him. "You're welcome. I was ready to ask you a hundred times if I needed to."

She laughed. "A hundred times? Really?"

"Oh hell yeah, and it would have been worth wrecking my knees getting down and begging each time. Don't you worry about deserving, baby. We deserve each other. I promise, Ben, I'm going to make you so happy you'll never want to leave the farm except for a few months a year for school."

"I believe you." She held on tight as he spun her around the kitchen. "And I'm going to change your world. By the time I'm done with you, you'll be so happy the cows' mooing will be the only thing to get your happily exhausted self out of our bed in the morning."

"I can hardly wait." There was laughter in his eyes, anticipation and pleasure there as well. "I love you, Ben."

"I know it! I feel it, I see it, I hear it, I taste it, I smell it." She pressed kisses to his neck and cheeks between her words. "I love you too. I'm going to take such good care of you, Mark. You don't even know."

"I do, that's why this is going to be a short engagement. I want to marry you before the New Year." His lips mimicked hers, finding her freckles and feasting.

"How's Christmas sound?"

"Like eight days too long," he admitted. "But it'll do, and if later on you want the big wedding we'll do that."

"Just you, I just want you." Ben pressed her mouth to his, the laughter ebbing for an incredible, tenderness-filled moment. "For the rest of my life, Mark Dougstat, I want you."

Chapter 14

Ben waited for her flat iron to heat up. Since she'd decided to do her own hair for the wedding, she'd had to carve out plenty of bathroom time to practice. Unfortunately, between getting finals ready and graded, she hadn't had much time to play with her options. With only a few days until the big 'W' she knew if she was going to do a decent job, it was time to pick a style.

At least she'd gotten the dress situation settled after a single shopping trip to Kansas City with Kira. That part had been easier than she'd expected, and she smiled when she looked at the dress bag hanging on the shower rod. Kira had tried to talk her into a prom dress, but in the end, they'd both been pleased with the more age and weather appropriate dress. Ben had asked for a clear bag just so she could look at it. It was the happiest gray she'd ever seen with an ice blue band around the waist, and it would be perfect for a Christmas wedding.

She wouldn't wear white, but she'd done that before and didn't need the big to-do again. Mark's mom wasn't making the trip north in December when she'd be up at Easter, so Mark wasn't pushing for a big wedding either.

It was all going to be sweet, she decided, tucking a piece of wallpaper back in place against the bathroom mirror. And the money they saved by not going crazy could be used to remodel.

Retro was in, but the antique bouquet pattern on the bathroom walls and floor had seen much better days. She looked forward to doing the little things around the house. It would be challenging to get Mark's house up to par, but it was a challenge she was up for.

She ran her hand over the flat iron and since it nearly burned her she picked it up and started taming her curls. She'd do it flat with a ribbon for the wedding. It would be simple, elegant and pretty.

"So you aren't coming?"

Ben winced when she heard Thomas's hard voice through the thin wall between the kitchen and bathroom. He couldn't see her behind the partially closed door. She didn't mean to eavesdrop, but he was loud and she couldn't help but overhear.

"You know, why the hell did I even think you guys would come? It's freaking Mark's wedding, Christmas and Kira's birthday is in a few weeks. Why not come and do it all at once, then you won't have to take us this summer."

There was silence, and Ben realized he was talking with one of his parents. From their history with the kids, she hadn't expected them to make the trip, but Mark had confirmed it when they'd been planning the reception. Her soon-to-be sister and brother-in-law didn't take time off for anything. For some reason she'd at least pictured them spending time with the kids when they were in France, but Mark had corrected that misconception with stories of random nannies. It was a wonder that Thomas and Kira weren't more bitter about their parents.

"So it's just not important enough. We're not important enough."

His words broke her heart. She hated how angry Thomas sounded, yet what was worse was the resigned tone he used. He hadn't expected to be surprised. It was a hard day when a kid had to give up on anything, be it Santa or in the worse case, their parents.

"Yeah, well, it's bullshit," he said and paused a moment. "Oh, do you really think you're going to tell me what to do? Ever? I mean, come on, I can swear all fucking day if I want to, and there isn't a damn thing you shit--"

"Thomas." She kept her tone gentle, but couldn't let him talk that way to anyone. Not even if she agreed with his assessment and theory about his parents.

"Whatever. Don't forget to send Kira a card."

He hung up hard, but not so much she had to get after him about it. She opened the bathroom door the rest of the way so she could see him. He looked defeated and defiant. Really, he looked like he was bracing for another emotional hit. Any kind of serious reprimand could be the piece to completely ruin Thomas's day, and even though Ben knew his attitude with his parents needed to change, she didn't have the heart to pursue it at the moment.

"I'm sorry for eavesdropping, but I was actually just going to yell for you. Do you, um, you don't happen to have any hairspray in your room, do you?"

The anger left his face slowly, shame and embarrassment replacing it. Ben's heart sank. She'd hoped to give him an out if he wanted it, not to make things worse.

"I don't, sorry, Ben," he said. "I'm sorry about the way I was talking. I shouldn't have said that stuff."

"No," she agreed, "you probably shouldn't have spoken like that to anyone. But sometimes when we're really frustrated and angry, things like that happen."

"I'm not sorry I said it to him." He was stubborn, something she rarely saw in Mark, but time had blunted some of the more volatile emotions in the older Dougstat. "I'm sorry you heard me saying it. Ladies aren't supposed to have to listen to that stuff."

"Honey." She had to stop a moment and think of what she needed to say. How many times when she was Thomas's age had she thought of saying something similar to her aunt? Something horrible and mean just to get the ugliness out of her system? Hell, she still wanted to do it at times. "We can't control other people. In fact, there is next to nothing in this world we have control over. Sometimes it makes us feel better to say the things that are on our mind. At least in the short term. But remember, Thomas, you are so much better than those ugly words and anger."

He shook his head. "They suck, Ben. If they'd even take two days off, just to spend a single day here, it would mean everything to Kira. I thought maybe since it would be Mark's wedding, Kira's birthday and Christmas all within days that they'd make the trip. It would be the first Christmas we ever spent together. Kira thought since the wedding and everything…"

He trailed off, and the reason behind his anger became glaringly clear. Kira wanted her parents to be close for Christmas, and she didn't have the years of disappointment Thomas did to know better than to ask. He wasn't angry for himself; he was crushed because he was going to be the one to tell Kira they weren't coming. It wouldn't be the first or last time she was sure.

"She asked me and Mark for two things this Christmas," Thomas continued. "She wanted to keep you, and she wanted our mom and dad to come for Christmas. Mark took care of the first part and I tried--"

"You did try," she interrupted. "You tried, and that's all you could do in this situation. We'll all make sure Kira has a really great Christmas."

"Now I don't know what to get her." He looked defeated. "I would have really liked to give her this one thing. It shouldn't have been a big deal."

It shouldn't have, but Ben knew he hadn't expected his parents to come, yet had hoped for a miracle. He'd probably prayed about it too and would deal with that faith question himself as well. It was hard to be sixteen with so much happening, but she was willing to help.

"You know, Mark wasn't the only one who helped with getting me for Kira. In fact, I'm pretty sure I'm getting the best part of this Christmas. I'm getting a whole family."

"Right, which Uncle Mark made happen." Thomas still didn't perk up. "I mean, I'm glad about it, but now I'm going to have to get Kira something really good."

He'd shared a lot of confidences with Ben in the last few minutes, and from the way he fidgeted she could tell he felt insecure. What sixteen-year-old boy didn't? They were going to be closer than that though. She was going to be his aunt and with adulthood coming fast, they needed a little common ground.

"I can't have kids," she blurted.

He looked up and cocked his head in question.

"I mean physically, my former husband and I tried, but I was never able to conceive, so chances are, babies aren't in my future. That's one of the reasons Mark was so special right off the bat. He had you and Kira and loved you so much, and I just thought it was wonderful that he'd raised such a nice, intelligent young man."

"Oh, and you did meet me first." Thomas's grin showed the cocky pleasure of the young man she'd come to know and love.

"That's right," she said. "Without you and your smarty-pants I don't know when Mark and I would have crossed paths. So technically I'd say you were the matchmaker and reason behind the wedding taking place in three short days."

He looked excited a moment, then his face fell a little. "Kira still won't get to see Mom and Dad."

She put an arm around his boney shoulder. "I know, buddy." He was tall, and for a moment he stiffened but then relaxed into a half hug. "We'll make Christmas good though. I bet you boys have made it a good day from her first year."

"And it'll be better with you here." The missing confidence was back in his firm reply as he turned the half hug into a full one. His arms squeezed her a little too tight, but it was nice.

"Okay." She pulled back before the tears she was fighting escaped her. They were close to the surface, and she didn't want them to soggy up the moment. "Well, if you don't have any hairspray I'd better get working on my hair. It's going to take a little longer without it."

"Want me to run to town and get you some?" he offered, always looking for another reason to drive.

"I don't think that's necessary." She laughed, and if he hadn't been so tall she would have ruffled his hair like the boy he was quickly leaving in the dust. "By the time you'd get back, I'd be done and it would be time for chores."

"I bet the cows would appreciate it if your hair had hairspray in it," he replied, his charm directly inherited from his uncle, and Ben laughed again.

"I'll tough it out tonight, but tomorrow morning you can be my chauffeur if you want to drive in with me to get groceries."

"Cool. We need fruit snacks."

Of course they did.

Chapter 15

The internet was one of Victoria's favorite things. From all over the world a person could get intimate community details with just the click of a mouse. She was able to keep tabs on old friends in New York City as well as in Chicago. Her new favorite was checking in on Flathead Falls. The news there was always thrilling.

Ben's car had been a mess of deliberate, unnecessary chaos according to the writer. Victoria grinned as she reread that wording and thought it suited her mission in life. 'Deliberate, unnecessary chaos.' It had a nice ring to it.

She giggled at the mention of chickens burning alive, animal cruelty cited in the list of charges for the culprit should they be caught. The sheriff's office was working diligently and would find exactly jackshit and that was okay with her.

If they did happen to find any evidence it would be from Steven, not her. It was his equipment and fingerprints that would have been left behind. She'd been snug as a bug in the car at the end of the driveway that night.

The thrill of her life had been when the light in the house turned on as Steven was rigging the bomb in the car. She'd actually seen Ben walk through the house and look out the window. For a split second she'd thought they were caught, and it had been a delicious second.

Lucky for Victoria, Steven was no longer an issue. The dumbass had mistakenly assumed she'd intended him to join her in her hideout. As if she would ever restart a life with a giant pile of fat and stupid. She'd let him believe he had a place in her life while he drove the car he stole toward Arkansas.

For about two minutes he'd been the big, strong man putting the little woman in her place. She'd let him drive, let him order for her at the cafes they stopped at along the way out of Missouri. Every time she played

Stephanie Beck

meek and mild, his dominance grew until as they were driving down the interstate, he'd demanded a blow-job. She'd given it without complaint, and he'd come with a shout and rough pull of her hair. When she'd looked up he'd been grinning.

It never ceased to amaze her how close stupid and mean were to sadism and homicide. He'd taken to evil like a fish to water, and she felt supreme satisfaction knowing she'd played a part in introducing him to the truth of his nature.

At least she had in the moments before she shot him in the face. It seemed right to destroy her creation. Really, she couldn't have thought of a better way to end their acquaintance. After all, he would never do better than her, and she didn't want him breathing any more of her air.

Destroying his mouth and both hands eliminated any chance of identifying the ravaged corpse she left somewhere on the back roads of Missouri. She'd waved goodbye and driven off to parts unknown.

Well, not too unknown, more like Las Vegas, and she loved it. For the last three months she'd been in the city that never stopped, where men were a dime a dozen and sex paid for nearly everything. If things got tight, she knew where to find the best johns and cash-heavy drunks after dark.

With the whole Bennie situation finally satisfactorily wrapped, Victoria was ready for bigger and better things. Maybe she'd head to Phoenix, once she had her nest egg built up. She loved the sand and heat. After living a year in Chicago she needed the heat to purge the dank, cold, and humidity. Maybe she could watch the kids hunt Easter eggs in the sand.

She flipped pages ahead in the Flathead Falls Forum, past the pitiful Thanksgiving Day parade, pausing at Christmas when the front page caught her eye. She stopped, cold fury growing with each word under the half-page picture. *Newlyweds Mark and Benfri Dougstat; Married Christmas Eve in a Sunrise Ceremony.*

It was unacceptable, absolutely unendurable. She read the article twice. The short announcement didn't give much information, but its very existence exposed her failure. The picture of the happy couple burned away every ounce of contentment Victoria had felt only moments before.

She couldn't possibly move on without finishing Bennie. It wouldn't be fair to anyone. They both deserved closure after all Don had done. Victoria's closure would be completely destroying anything that reminded her of the bastard. That included Bennie.

Victoria brought up a travel site and began to plan. Some things in life a person just had to accept and let go into the universe. Wiping out Bennie wasn't one of those things.

Chapter 16

"Uncle Mark! Aunt Ben, we're home!"

Ben was much too sated to care about the interruption. Three orgasms did that for her, but above her, determined for a fourth that just wasn't going to happen, Mark swore.

He liked pacing himself, and it was going to bite him in the butt this time. She held back a giggle as he groaned in frustration. He was at the point where he'd been holding back for so long he'd have to really focus to finish, and with the kids in the kitchen she knew that would be a challenge.

"Sorry, handsome." Ben gasped and tried not to laugh out loud.

"Where is everyone? Aren't Uncle Mark and Aunt Ben here? I saw his car outside and the truck. Why is their door shut? We haven't had dinner yet, so it's way too early for bedtime." Kira's voice carried like it always did, and Ben heard her backpack fall to the floor.

"Come on, squirt," she heard Thomas say, another clunk from the kitchen as he set his even heavier pack down. "They're probably taking a shower or something. Let's go outside. I saw kittens in the creamery yesterday."

"Kittens already? But I'm hungry." A cupboard squeaked and closed a little hard. "Okay, but then I want supper. Aunt Ben said we're having a roast, and I can smell it."

"So much for the vegetarianism, ya quitter. Come on, it'll take ten minutes," Thomas said loudly, and the door closed.

"I'm raising his allowance," Mark promised and leaned back on his heels. He looked Ben up and down, his eyes glowing in appreciation. With a big hand, he tapped against her hip. "Turn over, pretty girl."

"You are so romantic." She laughed and rolled over onto her knees, knowing full well his appreciation for her backside.

"You know it. Romance is my middle name." He moved up behind her, his hard hairy thighs tickling the backs of hers deliciously. His warm hands moved up and down from her shoulders to the small of her back, the calloused quality of his palms making her arch for more. "You aren't too sore, are you, honey?"

"Nope, whatever you've got, handsome, I want it." She rested her face in his pillow, breathing in the scent of him while he took his place and slipped inside. The position did very little for her, her favorites were on top or missionary where she got the most stimulation, but after three orgasms she was more than content to just enjoy the feel of him enjoying himself.

Being with Mark was always good. The newness and sweetness of every coupling more than made up for the moments of taking one for the team.

Ten minutes meant ten minutes, so Ben didn't demand any more finesse, knowing in that time she wanted Mark to finish, to have a shower, and to be able to get a start on finishing supper. She had papers to grade, and Kira had said something about a school project she needed help with. Thomas also had some things to go over from his guidance counselor.

"Hey." Mark smacked her butt just a touch more than gently, demanding the attention she was ashamed to have let wandered when he was doing such good work. "Pay attention, woman."

"I am, I am." She wiggled her butt and pressed her hips toward him. "You just spoiled me earlier, that's all, and the timing..."

"Okay, okay. Just keep thinking about me for another, ah, ah, damn, Ben."

She smiled into the pillow, loving the sounds he made during sex. He was vocal, loud even at times, and for a good ole farm boy who'd never gone beyond local, he knew sex and was really good at it. She already had a list of new favorites, and it grew nightly.

Since their wedding night he'd been making her completely happy and satisfied and made no show of slowing. The abstinence played a part in that, she figured, but it wasn't all. She would still want him in forty years, fresh from the pasture all sweaty and masculine and handsome.

He collapsed into her, never treating her like she might break, but always conscious of her needs and desires.

"Damn, you're a fine lay," he muttered, sinking his teeth into her shoulder before licking the sore spot. "Even your freckles taste good."

"Again, you say the sweetest things to me, husband. And did you just say my freckles *taste* good? You're so weird." She giggled and pinched the skin around his middle.

He jerked away, laughing too. Their affection-filled camaraderie was what she cherished above all else. Being a princess was great, but being his best friend, the one he wanted to laugh with, was priceless.

"They are delicious. How about this for sweet? I love you, wife." He kissed the bite spot and licked another freckle.

"I like it," she admitted, smoothing his hair with a sweaty hand. "I really do, and it beats the hell out of tasty skin blemishes. And I happen to be able to reciprocate the love and compliment on the laying skills."

"I'm glad you love me, and yeah, I am a good lay," he said breezily.

"I just can't wait to hear what you say next." She shook her head.

"How about 'if you let me get into the shower first, I'll do the dishes tonight'?"

"Okay, that one's iffy." The thought of dinner cleanup reminded her of how tired she'd been since she'd picked up an early morning tutoring session with a group of seniors. "You can have the shower first, but then you have to preheat the oven for the potatoes *and* wash the salad before dinner."

"Deal." He hopped out of bed with his usual stamina.

He wasn't a snoozer after sex. Cuddling and talking in afterglow were his favorite things, but if they did indulge in a quickie when they had the time, he had no problem jumping on to his next task. Even while she wanted to lounge and sleep off the high.

He turned to her on his way to the bathroom and grinned. "Rest up, beautiful. I've got plans for a repeat performance later."

She couldn't help the smile that held on even after he was out of sight. He was an amazing husband, every single thing he'd promised before they'd exchanged vows just before Christmas was proving true.

The ceremony had been perfect, mostly borrowed and lent, but Mark had butchered a beef so there'd been lots of good food and friends, and at the end of the day she'd gotten the best Christmas present ever. She relaxed in bed until the shower turned off and gave Mark a few extra minutes to dress. With spring break only two weeks away, she hoped they'd find more quiet afternoons for fun.

"All clear, sweetheart. I'm going to wash the salad and take the kids out to get a few chores done before dinner."

"All right. Thanks."

Lying in bed sounded great, but a hot, uninterrupted shower after the long day and sweaty lovemaking was too tempting to miss.

The smell of roasting meat was heavy in the air when she stepped out of the bathroom after her shower. An overflowing salad bowl sat on the counter, and even though Mark was already outside, the oven was on, so she added the potatoes. The roast she'd put in the slow cooker before work was nearly done, and she pulled a frozen apple pie from the freezer to bake while they ate.

Thomas and Kira often ribbed Mark about the better food since she'd moved in. It was funny because she'd never taken a whole lot of pride or pleasure in cooking, but having a very appreciative group of eaters made the mundane task more fun. She glanced out the window and saw Mark and the kids heading for the barn. It would take the potatoes a while to cook, so she wasn't worried about anything being ruined. He'd always been good with his time, but she liked to think his change in habits came from wanting to spend more of it with her. She often graded over her lunch break so she didn't have to bring work home. Maybe if she got a jump on the dishes while the potatoes finished, they'd really be able to have a nice evening together with the kids, followed by a repeat of their afternoon fun. With that in mind, she ran hot water into the sink with a smile.

Just as she transferred the beautifully roasted potatoes into a serving bowl, the back door opened. Laughter and the sound of running water soon followed, and Ben hurried to get the rest of the food on the table. Everyone was always happy to help, but a sudden urge to spoil them came over her. Since catching her latest cold, fatigue had dragged her down, so the idea of making dinner a little special made her smile.

The phone rang, but with her hands full, Ben let Mark answer it.

"Hey, Rick. We're just about to sit down for dinner, what do you need?"

She quickly set the table and giggled when Mark snagged her around her waist. It was a wonder she ever got anything done with him close by, not that she'd ever complain about his random showings of affection. He pressed kisses to the back of her neck, sweet reminders of their stolen time earlier, but when he started talking about grain again, she swatted his hands and escaped to finish putting dinner together.

It should have been the perfect meal, one of her favorites definitely, but even though everything looked amazing, Ben looked on with little appetite. She'd caught Thomas's cold and had been feeling crappy the past two weeks. Spoiling the family with a good dinner had been a nice thought, but now, her burst of energy gone, Ben wished she'd made herself a can of chicken noodle soup instead. She needed to get more hand sanitizer to protect her students from the mutant germs that kept latching onto her.

Kira plopped into her chair but stood quickly, giving Ben a hug before grabbing the ketchup from the refrigerator. How had she forgotten to add ketchup? They ate it on everything. Ben was still adjusting to watching them all eat their eggs with ketchup.

"Hey, Ben." Kira poured a huge dollop of red goop on her plate and grinned. "I got a perfect score on my spelling test again, so I get to move up to the advanced group."

"Good for you, kiddo. I knew you could do it."

Mark hung up the phone and sat, Thomas to his right, and Ben settled into her chair as well.

"I just needed someone to practice with, and Thomas is always busy and the letters jump around for Uncle Mark," Kira said. "There are only three of us, and we get to go to the enrichment room for an hour a week."

"That will be fun. How was your day, Thomas?"

"Fine." The teenager got the words out around a mouth full of potatoes.

"Melody's still sick," Kira added. "Mononucleosis."

"I know, poor girl. It's been a few weeks now, so hopefully she'll be feeling better soon. Mono is no fun at all."

The meal was a hit, and there wasn't even a single potato left in the bowl. Leftovers were rare at any meal, and even though Ben hadn't eaten much, Thomas had taken care of any excess. The pie turned out perfectly, and after helping themselves to giant pieces, Thomas and Mark volunteered to do what was left of the dishes.

After their own smaller desserts, Ben helped Kira with her spelling work. The girl's mind was like Mark's in her ability to memorize, but she was an auditory learner and did better hearing the words rather than reading them herself. Ben's students were working on projects, so she didn't have much for homework, which left her all evening to work with Kira as Mark spoke again with his seed provider.

After helping Kira with her bedtime ritual, Ben tucked her in and wished she too could head for bed, but it was too early. Thomas was in his room doing homework, but he'd probably stop by the kitchen for a bedtime snack before ten. Then he'd sleep too.

"Honey, I'm going out to check the calves. I'll be right back."

Mark's announcement drew Ben out of her envious bedtime thoughts.

"Okay, be careful," she called.

When the back door closed, Ben looked around the living room. She could tidy up a little, maybe even get a jump on the weekend cleaning spree she had planned. Instead, she grabbed a fleece blanket from the back of the couch and settled in, propping her feet on one of the throw pillows. Going to bed was tempting, but spending the last few minutes of the night alone with Mark sounded better. She checked the clock and turned on the news. He'd be back in twenty minutes. She could last that long.

* * * *

"Ben." Mark shook her foot when he found her asleep after the first weather forecast. "Honey, let's go to bed."

She usually woke well, but lately, with her early class and helping around the farm she was exhausted by the time the kids were in bed. Spring always proved to be a busy time for him, and truth be told, he was ready for bed as well. He'd have liked that second round of sex he wasn't going to get. When she just grunted and turned into the back cushions, bedtime was inevitable.

"Bet she's got mono."

Mark looked over and saw Thomas leaning against the wall with a huge sandwich in his hands. It was a triple-decker with peanut butter and bananas. At least that was what Mark could identify. These days, he was never sure what all Thomas put in his food. It made him shudder.

"I really hope not. You don't look like you have that problem." Mark kept his voice hushed even though his delicate bride slept like a log. "You're feeling okay, right?"

Thomas gulped hard, and his whole throat worked to force the food down. "Yep. Melody's mom said she's doing a lot better too, so I get to see her tomorrow after school if it's okay with you."

"That's fine if she's not contagious. It'll be good when she feels better. We've missed her around here." Mark liked Thomas's girlfriend. He didn't know if it would be one of those lasting high school romances, but for now Melody was a sweet girl who made Thomas smile and that was okay with him.

"Not contagious," he confirmed and took another huge bite, his jaw so extended Mark thought it cracked.

"Want some milk?" he asked dryly.

He watched as Thomas chewed half the sandwich in his mouth now. "We're out of milk," he muttered, skill keeping bread and bananas from flying.

"Okay, I'll pick some up tomorrow. Damn, boy, don't talk with your mouth so full, you'll choke."

Thomas finished chewing, opened his mouth to show it was empty and then grinned. "Sorry. Yeah, out of milk, bread, and cereal--I had to eat mine tonight with water."

"All right. Let's hope the hens feel like laying some eggs in the morning or we'll be eating hotdogs for breakfast. Goodnight."

Thomas headed up the stairs, waving as he went, and Mark turned his attention back to Ben, who was still sleeping soundly. He turned off the TV and hustled to the back door when he realized he'd forgotten to set the alarm. Things were quiet, but he wasn't going to be lulled into forgetting something like that.

"Okay, baby, come on." He leaned down and lifted her high to his chest.

She weighed less than two hay bales and felt a hell of a lot softer. He was a fan of having a wife, someone who smelled good and always had a smile for him. Even when she was mad, he knew it wouldn't be long before she was smiling and teasing him again. It was damn nice to be loved. Sure the kids loved him, his mom too, but Ben displayed a whole different set of feelings.

He was just himself, warts and all, and she loved him every day. That was a pretty heady feeling. He tucked her in their bed and headed for the shower once more because he'd had to free a calf from a sticky patch of muck. He needed to clean the stalls in the morning after chores. Ben was going to bitch on the way to work about how bad he smelled, and that thought made him grin.

* * * *

"Mark, for the love of God and all His angels, if you ever clean stalls before driving me in again, I'm not going to be held responsible for my actions."

He grinned as Ben hand cranked her window down, and he lowered his as well. Kira sat in the backseat, and Thomas too until his carburetor was fixed. Both had their shirts above their noses.

"Oh, come on, guys, it's not that bad."

"Adult cow poop is one thing, but calf poop is horrid," Ben assured him, keeping her face turned to the window. "Ick!"

"I'm a farmer, sweetheart," he reminded her, biting his cheek to keep from laughing. "To us folks living off the land, manure is the smell of money. Aren't you glad business is so...strong?"

"That is so gross in so many ways." She pulled her shirt sleeve to cover her face.

He just laughed and kept driving. The ride was about twenty minutes and mostly on gravel, which was why he never bothered washing his car or buying a new one. The dirt and rock would just eat a new finish. His old ruster with a good engine and tires would drive until it became so corroded it wasn't safe. So far at year thirteen he had high hopes for it to see twenty.

"Oh God, stop, stop," Ben groaned, and he looked over to find his wife deathly pale and gagging.

He pulled over and hit the brakes just in time for Ben to open the door and lose her breakfast. Kira yelled at him for stinking so badly he made Ben puke, and poor Thomas, who didn't do well around illness, reached for his own door.

"Ben, are you okay?" He was such an ass. It wouldn't have killed him to take off his shit kickers or throw on some fresh clothes for the ride to town.

"That was horrible. Oh no, Thomas, are you okay?" Ben asked, accepting the napkin Mark offered. "Sorry, buddy, I think I just got car sick."

"Uh uh, I bet it's mono," Kira predicted. "Melody thought she just had a tummy ache but bam, mono, and she was at our house."

"Oh, hell." Ben groaned and held her stomach a long moment. Mark walked around the car and helped Thomas back in the car, pale but okay. "Just what we need, huh, Thomas? A nice double case of mono at the house."

"I'll call and make an appointment for you for after school," Mark told Ben, handing her his coffee to rinse her mouth. "Are you sure you should go to school?"

"I'm fine. I'm sure I will be. What about Thomas?"

"He's a sympathy puker." Kira patted her brother on the shoulder. "That's one of the reasons he really can't visit Melody. Then her mom would have two pukers instead of one."

"Okay, Kira, that's enough 'puke' talk." Mark added a little smile to ease the rebuke. "Are you two okay for school, or should I just drop off Kira and tuck you both back in for the day?"

"I'm fine," Ben said.

He didn't like how shaky her smile was but he nodded.

"Me too, just don't throw up again." Thomas pulled out his iPod and tilted his head to the headrest with his eyes closed.

"I'll do my best," Ben said dryly, and Mark felt worse.

"And I won't clean the barn before giving you a ride again, honey," Mark promised and continued on, taking special care with the corners and stops to prevent either sore stomach from jerking around too much so soon after being sick.

Nine hours later he was back at the school. Thomas had baseball practice and Kira was at her friend's house to work on a project, so it was just him and Ben. Or it would be if she ever got her butt in the car. With their busy schedules sometimes the rides to and from school were the only times they really had to catch up. Spring planting was in high drive and Ben helped with that on the weekends and evenings, if she didn't have her own work to do.

"Hey, handsome." Ben plopped into the car, slamming her door behind her. "I'm pooped. Did you have a good day?"

He leaned across the seat. "I did." He kissed her forehead when she shook her head instead of offering her lips. "Were you sick again?"

"Just once right after I got in. Then I was fine all day, but I might have mono." She winced. "Well, you'll probably have it too, but why chance it?"

"I had mono when I was a kid, so hopefully it'll miss me this time. I made you an appointment at the clinic just in case you were still feeling rough. It's in five minutes." He pulled away from the curb and headed for the clinic as he filled her in. "I got you in with my doctor today and scheduled an appointment for Thomas on Saturday in case he needs it."

"That works. I like Doctor Harper."

* * * *

Mark waited in the clinic lounge while Ben did her doctor thing. She didn't like an audience during her visits, he'd found that out during the business with her leg.

He looked over the folder he'd brought. It held permission slips for a camping trip for Kira. His baby would be gone three days with her class, and it made his heart hurt to have her growing up.

He remembered when she was tiny and had spent hours trussed up to his chest or back as he did chores. While he wished Kira would stay his baby for a few more years, those days were numbered. Just like Thomas had taken the three day trip when he was his sister's age, Kira would too, and there was no going backward.

"Mr. Dougstat?"

Mark looked up at his usual nurse. "Hey, Cindy. Everything all right?"

"Could you come with me, please?" she asked, concern heavy in her expression, though she kept a smile on her face.

"Of course."

He started sweating on his way through the narrow clinic halls. It had to be bad news; only bad news required backup. He entered the exam room where Ben sat, visibly upset. The doctor looked furious with a thick file opened between them.

"Hi, honey. What's going on?" He took the seat beside her and held her hand.

"I'm--we're--it's not possible," she stuttered.

"Hi, Mark. What Ben is struggling with here is some misdiagnoses in the past," Dr. Harper explained.

The older man had been Mark's doctor for as long as he could remember and was a man Mark respected and trusted. He wouldn't have dreamed of sending Ben to anyone else.

"Misdiagnosis?"

"I'm pregnant. I can't be pregnant," Ben wailed. "I had tests. I had procedures. I was told I would not have children, that I could not have kids because... Well, damn it, it's all in the file."

"Ben," Dr. Harper said gently. "You obviously wanted to be pregnant."

"I did." The harsh denials turned to tears, and Mark fished for his hanky while the doctor handed over a box of tissues. "So much, but I can't be. Your test must be wrong."

"We did urine and blood tests," Dr. Harper said. "You are pregnant, and we'll do an ultrasound to confirm weeks. I have to tell you, that given these records, your age, and the timeline, your doctor ought to be beaten."

"Pregnant?" Mark looked between Ben and Dr. Harper, trying to decide who to believe.

"Don't get his hopes up," Ben snapped, tears falling down her cheeks. "He's such a good dad and should have a dozen kids, but this can't be true."

"Okay. Cindy, is the room ready?" Dr. Harper ignored Ben for the moment, and Mark knew he probably looked like a moron as he looked back and forth between the two, but to be fair, it was a pretty big shock.

"Yes, Doctor."

"Let's go." He scooped up the paperwork lying on the small desk between them. "Come on, Mark, drag her along if you have to. She's not going to believe she's pregnant until she sees the baby."

Five minutes later Ben's tears were back in earnest, because there was a baby on the screen. Two in fact. They were already taking recognizable, beautiful shapes, and Mark thought his hand was going to break under Ben's grip.

"There, pregnant." There was no missing Dr. Harper's satisfaction in the declaration. "Very pregnant, in fact, with two shy little ones. Let me get some measurements and I'll be able to tell you how many weeks along you are, but I'm thinking you're pushing four months."

"Wedding night babies," Mark said as he watched his babies kick and squirm on screen. "Damn, they're pretty."

"They're amazing." Ben's fingers dug into his forearm but he didn't care, too absorbed in seeing his kids. "Mark, I'm pregnant. Those are ours."

"They are." He pressed a kiss to her mouth, and she let him this time. "Not mono, huh?"

"Much better than mono."

An hour later they were on their way home with a copy of Ben's file in her lap. Dr. Harper had been adamant about malpractice on the part of her former physician and recommended she call the Chicago doctor immediately. She was flying too high to even think about all of the ugliness, and Mark hoped she'd stay that way for a while.

"I think I'm going to look through some boxes tonight," Ben said as they pulled into the long driveway. "Some of Don's papers I haven't gotten to yet are in there. Some of them are medical records."

"I'll help you," he offered. "Are they the ones in the basement?"

"Yeah, there are only two, so it shouldn't take me long."

"I'll pull out the grill and make some steaks since it's not too cold tonight," he replied. "I feel like celebrating."

"So do I. The papers can wait."

He could see she wanted to just let go and be excited, but he knew her better than that. "Nope, do it or it'll be on your mind. It'll take me an hour to get dinner together, so I'll get the boxes before I start. The kids and I will make dinner, and hopefully, you'll get a good chunk done before the food's ready."

"That would be great. Thanks, Mark."

"Of course, sweetheart. That should give you time to make some headway at least."

"Definitely. I'm sure I'll get a lot done." Silence stretched for a moment as he pulled up to the garage. "Then we can tell the kids about the babies."

"Tonight?" He smiled because the answer shined on her face when she turned to him.

"Absolutely."

Chapter 17

The damn boxes. In one box were forged tax receipts Ben would have to send to the detectives in Chicago since Don's case was still ongoing. They probably already had copies, but she'd foolishly kept the originals when she'd clung to hope of the detectives being wrong. The papers were nothing but an ugly reminder of her past, and she wanted them gone. The second box held Don's personal medical records.

Ben remembered him always going on about how doctors and insurance companies were just out to screw the layman, so he'd always paid cash and had personal copies of all his papers. A surge of affection bubbled up. His paranoia had always been one of her favorite traits. She flipped through the papers.

The old affection and humor died as she was reminded in black and white of all the lies he'd told. There was so much she hadn't known, and so much she didn't want to know. If he'd done half the things the police said, and she believed them, then her husband had been a very bad man. He'd hired killers, sold drugs to addicts and kids, and there was probably more the police had kept to themselves.

She set aside another phony checkbook. After she'd turned over of the paperwork, the police had informed her that all of the accounts were bogus. Don Mulenec. Muldany. Maverick. Mulligan. So many names for the man she'd adored. At least he hadn't used her name. Of all his sins, he'd stopped short from using her name and numbers. If it was a sort of honor she wasn't sure, but it was one less thing she had to fix.

With only one box to go, Ben didn't have a lot of hope of finding anything helpful. He'd had a knee surgery a few years before they met, an old tennis injury, he'd told her when she asked about the scar. It was the only major injury he'd ever had.

She'd been surprised when he'd been willing to see a specialist after years of trying to start a family. He'd always been so proud of being in good health that she thought his pride would get in the way, but he'd jumped right into the process of making a child. The doctor had done the fertility treatments at Don's prompting. He'd been willing to do anything to give her a family. The thought made her smile. He'd had to have some redeeming qualities. So far in her digging, he'd erred on the side of making her happy when it came to their life together. The police had even commented on it, and called her a spoiled wife.

She was just about to set aside the last box when she saw a hint of red at the bottom below a stack of yearbooks. She didn't remember any of them being red. His school colors had been green and gold, the fighting Irish. She pulled the books out and set them aside. The only thing remaining was a thin red binder, warped from the pressure of being under the heavy books.

She readjusted on the bed, tossing her pillow behind her back. On second thought she grabbed Mark's and tucked it under her knees as well. She was pregnant after all. The thought made her smile as she settled in again. The vinyl folder cracked when she opened it. She'd bet it hadn't been opened in years, and her curiosity intensified.

The first pages were medical records with her old Chicago hospital's letterhead. She flipped back to the first page, looked at the date, and frowned. Don's name was on it, but it detailed a surgery prep. She'd already found the record of his knee, so she looked closer.

The bill was mostly written in insurance code. Familiar words stood out occasionally, but it took a few more pages before she got to the itinerary. She stopped cold.

Vasectomy.

Ben looked at the date and the cold turned to ice. Two months before they'd married, so days after Don proposed, he'd had the surgery done. The paperwork was all there in black and white, his signature across the bottom giving his informed consent.

Any magnanimous feelings she'd entertained about him evaporated. He'd lied about everything. When she'd spent nights sobbing, he'd comforted her with promises he couldn't keep. There was no way they could have had a baby the natural or artificial way.

She looked through water-filled eyes and saw he'd declined to have any of his semen frozen. He'd never planned to have children with her.

The revelations only continued as she dug deeper. She'd thought the binder hadn't been opened in years, but that wasn't true. There were five letters at the back of the binder. She rubbed her cheek on her shoulder and pulled them out. They were crinkled, like he'd shoved them in as an afterthought. She didn't want to read them but with shaking hands she carefully straightened them.

The letterhead was from a different facility, and she let out a sigh of relief. She wasn't sure she could handle reading anything more about his vasectomy. Every time she came across the word her heart ached with the memory of all the failed treatments and lies.

The relief was short lived, however, when she read the sender's name. The letters were correspondence from her fertility doctor. Each was worse than the last, detailing the negative side effects of her treatments. They'd been side effects she'd been willing to risk at the time if it meant having a baby. According to the letters, the doctor had known there was no chance, and he'd tried to convince Don not to sanction the treatments.

Weight gain, hormonal imbalance, cancer. The list of possible problems needed an entire sheet of paper. Yet, the month before Don's murder, they'd been in Dr. Miller's office for more treatments. It was worse than she'd ever imagined, and with one last, sickening thought she yelled for Mark.

* * * *

"Hell." Mark swore when he found Ben sitting on their bed, even more pale than she'd been in the car. "I shouldn't have let you do this, not today."

"I should have gone through them before we got married. Did I even know the man I was married to for six years, Mark? Where the hell was I when all of this lying and scheming was happening?"

"What did you find, honey?" He gently closed the door behind him and sat beside her, trying to be calm because she wasn't.

"He had a vasectomy." Disbelief and pain filled her voice as tears gathered in her eyes. "We talked about kids, Mark. He said he wanted them. The whole time we were trying--I was trying, I guess--he was so supportive. He'd come home with lists of baby names, giving me hope when there was no way, no way, and he knew it. How could he do that to me?"

"I don't know, baby." He moved behind her back to cuddle her to him. "Did he have any close friends? Someone we might be able to call about this?"

She handed him a stack of papers. "The doctor who performed the vasectomy was the same one who did all of our fertility testing. He said the problem was all me. He lied."

"Okay, we'll call him first thing tomorrow when his office opens, and we'll get some answers." Anger wasn't going to help, but he was pissed.

The only remedy besides driving to Chicago and kicking the doctor's ass after he dug up Don and burned him, was taking action for Ben.

"Those treatments...Mark, they hurt. They flooded my body with hormones every month. They were expensive too, tens of thousands of dollars, and they all failed. I cried for hours." Her voice broke in a sob, the tears falling. "That--that bastard comforted me, told me he loved me anyway and we would have a baby one day. Was that a lie or was--was he going to steal one? You know what I hate?"

"What, honey?" He pressed a kiss to her hair, wishing he could hold her even closer and take her pain away.

"I had in-vitro done. It failed. Whose baby was it? I felt like such a failure. I couldn't even make my body support an innocent little baby who was already started."

"We'll get our answers tomorrow. I promise," he swore. "Easy, honey, I don't want you to get sick again, keep breathing."

"I feel sick." She cried harder, despite his calming words. "I feel sick all the way to my soul. How could he hate me that much? Even after all the lies and the ugliness, I still loved him because of the way he treated me. He was always sweet, always good to me, supportive and kind and--and how can it not all be a huge, ugly lie?"

Mark held her close as she cried miserably. He couldn't imagine such a bone-deep betrayal. Nothing in his life equipped him to commiserate, but he only held her tighter. To be on the receiving end of her love and not treat it like it was the most precious thing on Earth boggled his mind. What the hell had Don been thinking?

"I'm sorry, Mark." She turned in his arms and returned his hug. The papers were tossed aside as she tried to crawl under his skin. "I'm so happy about our babies, and I love this world I have with you. I shouldn't get so upset about something in the past."

"You get upset about anything you want." He brushed aside her hair and kissed her forehead. "I love you, and this hurts you. I'm going to help you deal with this the best I can, so you can focus on our babies."

"You're so good." She sighed but it was skewed by a hiccup. "You're too good for all of this."

"Nope, just a man, and I'll always help you. Now how about some dinner? I'll bring it in here and we can figure this out."

"No, let's go out to the kitchen. I still want to tell the kids about the babies." She wiped away the tears and gave him one more kiss before sitting herself up. "That was the plan, and I loved that plan."

"You'll still be pregnant tomorrow, sweetheart," he pointed out, planting a hand on each of her hips to help her find her feet.

"Yeah, and I'll most likely still be crying tomorrow too. I think you should start this pregnancy by giving me whatever I want, dear husband. Isn't that what the doctor said?"

He was glad to see her humor returning. He should have known it couldn't stay buried under the grief and sadness. For all the ugliness, their life was too bright for Ben not to emerge.

"You're right, honey. What was I thinking?"

Chapter 18

Ben loved random spring days off, and the district had a few. She spent the morning in bed being pregnant while Mark drove Thomas to a baseball tournament and Kira to a science day camp. Ben lolled in her happy place, enjoying just being in their big, soft bed, surrounded by the masculine mix of Mark's cologne and fabric softener that clung to his pillow. She loved the man, loved their life, and with the pregnancy she believed anything was possible.

How could it not be when she was married, step-mother to two great kids, doing a job she loved, with a farm full of animals and excitement to come home to at night? To top it all off, she had not one but two beautiful babies due by Halloween.

They would be peas she'd already decided, two peas in a pod, while she and Mark would be farmers. Kira would most likely be a Barbie of some kind, and Thomas probably a football player, so he could take his sister trick-or-treating and still get candy.

Only months before she wouldn't have believed so many beautiful things were possible. Victoria, that stain on humanity, was still waiting at the sidelines, but they were doing what they could with her. Mark had already called the sheriff to get patrols started again. The security system had been updated twice and video had been added.

They were paying out their nose for their own security. It was worth it, though, because Mark had a feeling, and his feelings were important.

"Hey, Mama."

She looked up to find the man on her mind in the flesh leaning against the door frame.

"Feeling lazy this morning?"

She opened her arms in an invitation he instantly accepted. "Yep. Pregnant women get to be lazy sometimes, you know." With him in her arms she let out a happy sigh. "Kids okay?"

"They are. I've got Thomas's coach watching for him, and I delivered Kira to Marisa Danahe."

"She's a type-A personality bitch." Which met all of Ben's requirements for a good temporary caregiver at the moment.

"She won't let the kids out of her sight. So are we getting business done right away? I want this garbage finished so we can enjoy the day."

"Okay. Let's just do it in here since my extension phone has more flexibility." It was a concession he'd made when the security team suggested it. "Speaker phone."

"Fine." He eyed the phone like he did most electronics, with distrust.

He did fine on his computer, on programs he was familiar with, but Ben knew he preferred his old corded phone and she loved him for it. She found Dr. Miller's phone number and called, setting the phone to speaker through the nurse's greeting and the hold music. She hummed and winked at Mark, holding his hand as they waited.

Her tension tried to build as each minute passed. With Mark beside her, one hand in hers, the other rubbing her stomach, she was able to stay relatively relaxed.

"Mrs. Wiggert. It's nice to hear from you," Dr. Miller greeted. "What can I help you with today?"

"My name is actually Dougstat now, Doctor Miller." Before all the revelations she'd had a good relationship with her doctor, but things had changed. "I remarried."

"Oh, I see." His less than jovial response spoke volumes to Ben, and she gripped Mark's hand harder. "What can I do for you, Mrs. Dougstat?"

"I've been looking into Donald's files. He kept extensive ones, you know." On the other end the doctor started cursing profanely, but she continued, "Do you think you'll be able to clear a few things up?"

"You aren't getting more than a hundred thousand from me," Dr. Miller said flatly. "I've already eaten the costs from your treatments and the in-vitro. I'm not letting you take anymore from me."

"Why were you treating me for problems I didn't have?"

"I had gambling debts." Dr. Miller sounded weary. "A lot of them, and somehow that asshole bought them from my bookie. It was unethical, but Don did things to people who didn't pay. A hundred grand. That's all you're getting from me."

"Having better luck with the gambling these days?" Mark asked sarcastically.

"Who is that?"

"I'm Ben's husband, and you have to know malpractice, willful malpractice cases like this one, are settled for millions." Mark's tone dared the doctor to argue. "What's a Chicago judge going to say when he finds out you were scamming a young woman in regards to fertility and her health?"

"A hundred and fifty is the most I'll offer. The treatments alone were well into the hundred thousand range with all the drugs."

"Drugs that weren't necessary," Mark shot back with passion she'd rarely heard from him. "Drugs that'll probably give her cancer in twenty years, you bastard. Who else have you done this sort of thing to?"

"No, God, no one. I'm a good doctor, but I have a family. Don would have killed me. He killed Sam Sherman for not paying him back on time. I've got three kids. You have to believe me. How can we settle this?"

"We'll be in touch," Mark said darkly.

"Good, talk to some people, get a number that is reasonable. I promise you, if I hadn't been afraid for my life and my family's lives I would not have done those treatments. As it is, I gave her half doses of the hormones, enough to have immediate side effects, but hopefully none long term. I didn't want to hurt her," he insisted.

"The in-vitro?" It was a question she didn't want the answer to. The possibilities had kept her up most of the night before.

"It wasn't fertilized." He still sounded irritated, but there was some gentleness in his words. "Don did not want children, not at all. But he wanted you, so that's why he went through this. He loved you in his twisted, psychotic way, and he wasn't going to share you. He told me that when I asked why he was going to such extremes."

"I see." But she didn't. She didn't think she'd ever understand.

* * * *

"We'll be in touch." Mark didn't wait for the doctor's response, just pressed the red button he assumed was the off switch.

They sat in silence for a long minute, Ben looking at the phone, sorrow in her face. He knew she had been holding out for something good in her former husband, something about him that deserved her love. Don had treated her well, and it hadn't been a lie, but it had been a manipulation. He hadn't just wanted her love, he'd wanted control. He'd wanted an angel only for him, and he'd lied and cheated, all at Ben's expense.

He bet Don wouldn't like that she was hurting. Wherever he was now, if he could watch, Mark figured the other man was angry at the fallout. He might have been crazy, might have been sick, but everything Mark was finding out, showed the other man had loved Ben. It wasn't a healthy love, but love in probably the only way Don had possessed.

"Well." Ben carefully stacked the papers back in order. "I think I'm going to call an attorney in KC and see what I can find out. I don't want to spend the next few years in court over this."

"That makes sense. We'll do whatever you want," he promised. "Do you want me to call my lawyer and see who he recommends?"

"Sure, that would be nice. Thanks." The words were right, but she didn't look at him. Finally she pressed the heels of her hands to her eye sockets. "I hate this, Mark. He really was crazy, wasn't he?"

"I think so," he said gently. "But, honey, in his way he loved you."

"So he cheated on me for years and lied to me about every damn thing? How is that love?"

"This isn't your fault. I bet in his head, he justified everything he did as long as he kept you happy in the process," Mark explained. "It sounds like he was a sociopath or at least someone who could justify anything. I don't know what you need to hear to feel better about this, Ben."

"I don't know either." She blew out a heavy, shaky breath and held her hand in a fist of frustration over the papers. "This was his one saving grace, you know?"

"Yeah, I see that. But it was Don's failure in all this. Never yours." Mark moved her to his lap, because he couldn't stand even the small separation anymore. "I know how you love. You love with everything you've got. He was a fool for abusing that. It's safe with me, always safe with me."

"Oh, Mark." She sighed and rubbed her tears on his t-shirt shoulder. "You've got a way with words, don't you? You make me feel like I'm everything to you."

"That's the way I want you to feel." He kissed the dark curls resting on her ear then tucked them behind the lobe like he often saw her do. "You're everything to me, Ben. For the rest of my life it's you and me. We've got babies to spoil, kids and teenagers to raise. There's no one I'd rather have at my side than you."

"I believe you." When she pulled back her red-rimmed eyes were teary but smiling. "I do, and together we're pretty great, aren't we?"

"Yep." He rubbed his nose against her red one. "Let's get this done, honey. We'll make some calls and settle this so it doesn't consume our lives."

"Not when there are so many other wonderful things to focus on right now," she agreed, sniffling deeply. "Thanks, Mark."

* * * *

Mark called his lawyer, who put them in touch with the best, and it only took Mark a moment to figure out the woman was a shark. She was also heavily into women's advocacy and the numbers she quoted were astronomical. Ben hadn't thought Dr. Miller would agree, but Susan Carmichael asked her to trust her.

It shocked him how quickly the matter was settled. Within a week of the first call, Mark and Ben had a new account at the bank in town with so many zeros at the end they both were a little nervous just to have it there.

He was still stacking hay bales, though. He didn't see the money, no matter the amount, changing the way he lived his life, and Ben wasn't making any changes in hers either. She was at school, had driven his car in that very morning. The money was amazing, but it wouldn't fix the past, wouldn't change what had happened.

He tossed another bale on the stack and took a seat, wiping his brow against the heat. Their first crop of hay had come early. It wasn't a good one, but it had been worth the few days he spent cutting, raking and bailing. It would make the second cutting much better.

Better. Everything seemed better this spring than any other one in the past. Married, kids were good, and babies on the way. He smiled as he pictured Ben before work. She'd been frantic because her pants, none of them, had fit. She'd confessed to wearing her 'fat pants' the last few weeks but had assumed it was newlywed weight.

It had been a joy for him to run out to his car at five in the morning and fetch the tote filled with maternity and baby clothes one of Kira's friend's mothers had sent. He'd known Kira couldn't keep a secret, and the women who had been his greatest help for years had been thrilled for them.

Ben had a shopping trip planned for the weekend. She hadn't shared it, but she'd been worried about money first thing after the excitement had set in about the babies. With the settlement money, she'd paid off Don's debts, and Mark had seen a weight lift off her after she'd sent those checks.

There would never have been an issue in getting her the things she needed. He would have seen to that before he allowed her pride to limit herself, but he knew what it was to take care of himself. Ben wanted that, and he was happy as hell she was finally able to support her needs with the honest wage she made.

Ben wanted to take Kira shopping too, and as far as money went, he had to buck up and let that part of their life mix more. He leaned back against the bales and swatted a spider when it crawled across his chest. Changes. Lots more than he'd expected, but then, what had he expected out of life?

He'd asked to be surprised on more than one occasion. He'd asked God to give him the strength to deal with whatever came next, and he had to smile. When life had started throwing him curves, it had also thrown him Ben.

Thunder rumbled from outside the barn walls. Mark jumped up and pulled his cellphone from his pocket as he looked out into the clear blue sky. They were coming into tornado season. He dialed the weather service to find a storm was predicted for in the next ten hours. Which meant if he was going to finish the hay, he had to get moving.

* * * *

Ben grinned when Mark flopped theatrically on the couch. He'd been stacking hay bales when she got home, and it hadn't broken her heart when he'd forbade her from helping with the heavy, hot work. She'd had a nice evening with the kids and since the weather was decent, she'd even spent an hour playing catch in the yard.

Kira was considering joining Little League, and Ben offered to help her practice her throwing and catching skills. Thomas had joined them after a few minutes, and she had some special time with the kids she thought of as her own.

They were an interesting little family, and she really hoped they would be huge one day. Both Thomas and Kira were excited about the babies. There was no doubt in Ben's mind there was plenty of love to go around, even if space was at a premium.

"So." Mark interrupted her thoughts with a playful flick at her pajama top. "Are these your super-sexy, made-for-husband-tempting fleece pajamas?"

"Can't you tell?" she teased.

He unsnapped the top button, opening the fabric an inch. "There." He looked much too pleased with himself. "Now they're your sexy jammies."

"I am a little naughty."

He winked, but then his face fell. His expression looked pained for a moment. "I've been wondering."

"What?" She frowned at his hesitancy.

"Am I naughty enough for you, Ben? I mean, you talked about toys and all sorts of stuff before we got married. We can do that, don't get me wrong, but I don't even know where to start."

She thought about that. In her underwear drawer there was a perfectly good vibrator being neglected. It had crossed her mind once or twice to break it out to add to the fun, but Mark always distracted her before she got up. Solo time didn't hold much appeal anymore. Not when a wonderful sexual experience was always only a few hours away. Being with Mark consumed so much of her mind that the perks of toys didn't come into the equation.

With him looking at her with such earnest embarrassment, she looped her arms around his shoulders and smiled. "Have you heard anything but sighs, screams and panting, lover boy?"

He grinned a little. "You do make a lot of noise. I love that."

"And I love every single thing you do that has me making them. We've got lots of time for toys and games, Mark." The rightness of the words settled in, and she knew they were true. "Yeah, we've got time for games. For now I'm very happy with our sex life."

"Good. If that changes or if you want anything more, promise you'll say something." His expression showed he was more worried about the situation than she was.

With such worry on his face, she couldn't help but want to ease some of his angst. The lights were out and the kids were sleeping, and given the topic of conversation…she undid another button. Then another and another. She watched his eyes follow the path of her skin and with each inch his worry eased and his grin replaced it.

"How about sex on the living room couch?" she asked, tugging the sleeves down her arms. "Can you handle that brand of naughty?"

She watched him covertly check the clock and up the stairs as well and bit back a smile. He was trying his damndest to be a little naughty, but her reasons for loving him stemmed from the practical side he was showing at the moment.

"Oh yeah, sweetheart, I'm always up for this brand of naughty."

The couch cushions sucked her deep when Mark settled on top of her. She hooked a leg over the back of the sofa and hugged him close, cradling him between her thighs.

"Are you feeling up to this, honey?" he asked, the kind, caring man she adored there even when he was attempting naughty.

"Oh, definitely," she promised, lifting her hips to rub against the hard erection his jeans were blocking. "But I'm thinking to do this right, both of us are going to have to lose our pants."

"Good point."

She hated to have him move away, but she let him go and he stood. She watched him shimmy off his jeans, the denim tight enough to mold his strong thighs and butt. Oh, and what a butt. When he turned away from her, just to undress, she realized he'd done it on purpose. With a laugh she reached out and smacked the flesh of his ass. He jumped a little but turned back with a grin.

"Really? Smacking the ass of the man who's going to make you scream?"

"Well, seems like there's a wee bit too much talking and not enough screaming…"

He growled and when he dove on her she laughed until his mouth descended on hers. Then all the giggles were gone, replaced with the deep, inner longing to be pleased just as he'd promised. Mark had forgotten her pants, but since they were stretchy they came off easily without Ben having to give up touching him. The scratchy fur of his legs always thrilled her, the obvious differences in his maleness enough to make her wet and even more ready.

The rocking always drove her nuts. He wasn't inside her though, he only teased as his tongue did the thrusting and exploring in her mouth. Her hips moved on their own accord, trying to coax him into the spot she needed him most. His cock slid through the moisture, so close to entering, yet he slipped by, teasing the top her clit with the firm, pliable tip of his penis. For a split second she thought about her toys and how fantastic it would feel to have one inside her as Mark teased. How much closer would she already be to climax if only she had exactly what she wanted?

"Mark, maybe we could--"

He slammed in, the teasing so abruptly over she couldn't even finish her plea. She tried to throw her head back and let the orgasm flow through her, but the sofa held her in place. She looked up and the grin on his face, though tight, told her everything. The tease.

Two could play that, she thought, the smugness on his face far from a turn off, but still, even in her orgasm haze, the challenge was made. She clenched him tight, trapping his cock inside her. He groaned and pushed in deeper, eliciting the same response from her.

Ben gasped with every thrust, keeping her vagina as locked as possible. She'd trapped herself in her own game. The second she released she was going to go off like a firecracker, but this time she wanted to come with him. He moved harder, faster and she bit her lip to make herself last. Just another moment, just another.

"Damn it, Ben, come for me."

She screamed but his mouth trapped it in an instant. Through her pleasure she felt his warm wetness add to hers with long spurts and pulls of his cock. The scream turned to a moan as she relished the feel of him inside her. There was nothing like it, not in the whole world. He pulled out and she wanted him back, but he didn't go far, snuggling beside her as he spread a throw blanket over their naked bodies.

"Wow," she said. "It gets better every time. That was… Hell, Mark, you're tricky."

"I know," he replied, sounding all too pleased with himself, but since he'd fulfilled his promise to make her scream, she figured he'd earned it. "But to be fair, you were the temptress in all this. Women who wear fuzzy bunny pajamas and leave the top button undone… Well, I know what to get you for next Christmas now."

"More slutty, fuzzy bunny pajamas?" She yawned through her giggle.

"Absolutely," he answered solemnly. "And maybe some with clouds too."

Chapter 19

Every damn year it was the same thing. The kids were at baseball, Ben too, and since it was quiet Mark decided to take care of the ugliest necessary evil of his adult life.

Taxes.

He had a guy who did them, but he still had to get everything together. If he kept better records throughout the year, he wouldn't have to spend hours in hell every spring, but did he plan ahead? He'd intended to, but then he'd met Ben and he'd been busy with other things.

At least all he had was the last half of the year to document and search. Tax exempt vs. write-off. Then there was the business with the kids. He was their guardian, but every year the same damn drama came up when overseas revenue came from Pierre and Kimmy. So he had to get all his court and custody documents together before he could hope to file.

He and Ben had decided to file separately, her economic status a whole kettle of fish he was thankful he didn't have to touch. Ben's lawyer had handled a lot of it, and Mark couldn't hope to follow it all. That still left him to do his own for the farm.

The file he pulled out was a spreadsheet from the feed store for his grain purchases for the year. It might as well have been gibberish. Until he gained his bearings on a page and forced himself to recognize the numbers and re-write them in the correct order, check and double check, they would remain that way. What should have been adding twelve numbers on a calculator turned out to be a ten minute job from hell.

The phone rang and he happily accepted the reprieve, leaving the damn papers for a moment. "Hello?"

"Is this Mark Dougstat?"

"Yes. Who is this?" The voice wasn't familiar, but that didn't mean much. Grain companies and crafters called pretty regularly to ask questions.

"I'm an old friend of Bennie's," she replied. "Is she in at the moment?"

"I'm afraid not," he answered, and when he looked out the kitchen window he saw a car pass slowly. He frowned. "Who is this again? I can take your name and number if you'd like."

"Oh no, I'll try later, don't worry."

Weird, he thought as he hung up. Ben's friends from work called once in a while, but...just weird. He sat at the table and forced himself to work. He was perfectly aware of the severity of his dyslexia. Most days it didn't bother him. The three-inch stack of invoices, bank reports, and receipts assured him this day would be an exception.

"Oh, my goodness."

Deep in thought and transcribing, Mark jumped at Ben's exclamation. He looked over his shoulder and dropped his pencil as she awkwardly hopped on one foot.

"What the hell happened?"

She looked up and smiled at him when he put a bracing arm around her shoulder. Pain was something he was pretty familiar with in their short history, and he saw the pinched lines around her eyes even though her smile was as beautiful as ever.

"I twisted my ankle at Thomas's game. It started swelling, not like I could tell since I've gained so much weight, but Sara Watson told me to come home and ice it. She's going to take the bunch out for ice cream after and drop them off before dark. I love country life. We don't need times, we just need a relative knowledge of the sun."

"Is it the same side you broke? That's probably why it's swelling more." He lifted her carefully, grinning when she squealed a protest.

"Mark, I'm huge. Don't you dare hurt your back."

"You still weigh less than a big bale, darlin' and you know I can lift two," he told her. "And your doctor said it's all baby. Babies."

He settled her at the kitchen table and put her foot on an empty chair.

"We'll ice it and if it comes down well, we'll call it a sprain. If not, we'll head in to urgent care and have it checked."

"Oh, we will not," she scoffed. He heard papers shuffling as he searched for an ice pack. "What's all this?"

Her tone had cooled, and it hit him that his desire for privacy in stumbling through his paperwork might look deceptive to her, especially after her ex. They'd discussed what she'd had to do in the aftermath when all of Don's dealings came to light, and Mark knew a table full of papers was sure to trigger bad memories.

"Just taxes." He pulled out Thomas's old favorite ice pack covered in faded ninjas and tried to stay casual. "Nothing big, just doing receipts so Bernie can do the paperwork next week."

"Bernie? Is there a tax guy out there who isn't named Bernie?" Ben laughed but he heard the tension still there. Considering her past, she did an admirable job with trust, but he could see they were on thin ice. Ice he needed to shore up so his pregnant bride didn't question his motives. Ever.

"Yeah. Actually, I got started and I was thinking, why the hell am I doing this alone?" The words killed his pride.

If a task presented itself, then he believed wholeheartedly God gave him the strength to complete it. This time the task was multifaceted. Marriage, he was learning, was one of God's greatest tools in love, duty, and humility.

"Oh? Are you just going to have Bernie do it?"

"No, I was going to ask you." He knelt before her, draped a towel over her swollen foot, and then wrapped the ice pack around. "I thought we could work together on it and get it done in half the time."

"Really?" She looked hopeful and doubtful at the same time.

The combination broke his heart, because he saw it slip at her more vulnerable moments. She wanted so much to believe she was safe with him, and for the most part, he believed she knew it. Insecurities were dirty monsters, though, and even he had his moments where he wasn't sure he was doing the right thing.

"Think you can help me, honey?" He slid the folder closer with the worksheet Bernie had sent. "I just need to calculate the receipts and fill in all this stuff. If you work the calculator, I can get things in order for you."

Her smile was too bright, and Mark thought he saw tears gather but nothing fell. His wife, so sensitive. Without another word, she started working the calculator.

Part of him unclenched and he realized how much he'd been waiting for her reply. She'd said she wouldn't push and that he could ask for help without them talking of why. Keeping her word had put to bed another fear. He retook his seat across from her and put the invoices together.

She wasn't the only one with insecurities, but more than ever his confidence in their relationship grew. Perfection didn't have a place in their home or obviously the doors would've been closed for him long ago. Mark smiled as he put another phone bill in a stack and brushed hands with Ben as she reached for it. Perfect or not, life still felt pretty damn good.

Chapter 20

"Come on, Ben! It's time for the three-legged race!" Kira shouted, tugging her when the game was called.

Ben bit back a groan as she let herself be pulled to her feet. Her ankle was better, so she couldn't even use that as an excuse. She was glad they were there, but wanted to put her swollen feet up while in the shade. The whole summer was left for her to expand and sweat, but both of those things were better in the shade.

"Come on, squirt." Mark hooked Kira up by her armpits and tossed her over his shoulder. He grinned. "You don't want Ben on your team right now. She'll just slow ya down with her big belly. She can cheer and get ice cream cones for the winners."

"Which will be us, right?" Kira squealed.

"It better be." He laughed and winked at Ben when she mouthed her thanks.

She caught sight of Thomas helping one of the moms at the ice cream stand and glided over. She'd already gain twenty pounds, most of it really the twins at nearly six months along, but anyone who mentioned waddling was a dead man. Ducks waddled. She glided, damn it.

"Hey, handsome," Ben greeted her nephew after he handed a sloppy vanilla cone covered in sprinkles to an equally messy first grader. "What's the special?"

"Root beer floats," he answered, already scooping ice cream into plastic cups. "I hate doing cones. If you want one, Mrs. Ribins will have to do it or it'll look like that kid's."

"Okay, two root beer floats, one with chocolate sauce, please," Ben requested and looked to the mom in the stand.

"He's doing fine." Patty Ribins smiled fondly. "How're you feeling, Ben?"

"Fine, really good actually since Mark got me out of the three-legged race. I can barely handle my own these days, an added one makes me nervous."

"He's a wonderful uncle," Patty said, and again Ben was reminded how much Mark did for the community.

"He's more of a dad." Thomas's admission surprised them both as he poured root beer. "We've got him broken in for the twins, right, Ben?"

"Yeah, you two have done a wonderful job teaching him how to be a good dad," Ben said, feeling a little gooey sentimental. "The best I'd say."

Patty handed her a napkin, and the look on her face said she thought the teenager was the sweetest thing too.

"We, me and Kira, were thinking that maybe we'd better call you and Uncle Mark 'mom' and 'dad.'" Thomas's words were a little rushed as he stayed busy pouring root beer and not looking at either of them. "You know, so the twins don't get confused."

"Oh, I see." Ben didn't have to ask for more napkins, Patty just handed over a wad. "I would be thrilled with whatever you two think is best on that front. I love that I'm your Aunt Ben. I'd love it if you thought to call me mom too."

"Okay, I'll talk to Kira tonight." Thomas handed over the two floats, heavy on ice cream and root beer, chocolate syrup on one, but didn't meet her eyes. "I don't know how you can eat it. I barely care what food tastes like, but that is not good."

"I know." Ben tried very hard not to cry. Thomas had brought the subject up like he had to avoid a scene, she was sure, but it was hard to hold back. "Thanks, Thomas. It's perfect, just how I like it."

"Oh, you're welcome." The praise had him blushing all the way to his ears. He was such a modest, funny boy. One day he was going to be an amazing man. "I think the race is starting."

"Okay, thanks. I can't miss it." She hurried away with Thomas's earnest, sweet words in her mind.

They wanted to call her 'mom'. Sure, they said it was for the twins, but that was an excuse. She wondered how long Thomas had thought of Mark as his dad. Probably as long as Kira had. They called their parents by their first names, so the titles were unclaimed.

She wanted to claim them so much, and she knew Mark would feel the same.

When she made it back to the open field, the racers were tied up, lined up, and waiting for the flag to drop at the end of the thirty-foot course. All the adults were male, and Ben could almost bet Mark had started that trend. There was a healthy competitive edge to the men, and it transcended into their kids as well.

"Hey, Ben. Ben!" Kira yelled. "Look!"

"I see," she called back, nodding at the pink strip around their legs. "Go, Mark and Kira!"

The elementary field was teeming with people. Students, parents, grandparents, and employees from kindergarten through sixth grade had gathered to enjoy a beautiful day. Ben watched the elementary school secretary, who looked like a first grader herself, so small and slim, raise one hand. The racers moved to attention. Then she raised the other hand, gave her hips a little shake to the children's amusement, and finally jerked them straight down.

The shot came from the left. The dads stopped the kids. Every adult, it seemed, had a child suddenly behind them as they searched for the cause of the startling gunshot.

Ben's blood ran cold when she found the only person moving in the crowd. Another shot rang out. There was really nowhere to hide, nowhere to escape the shots, but so far no one had been hit.

The kids from the race ran to their mothers after their dads quickly untied them. Cellphones were pulled out all over, and Ben knew whatever came next was sure to be horrible.

"Bennie!"

That voice. Ben recognized it from the dozens of phone calls. Even though she hadn't heard from the stalker in months, it was her voice Ben heard in her nightmares, and now the nightmare was reality.

"Bennie!" Victoria screamed again, her long, platinum hair bright against the sapphire blue cocktail dress she wore, complete with five-inch stilettos. "Oh, Bennie! Vicki's here."

Ben had nothing to defend herself, and the people around her were in the same boat. They were stuck until the police arrived. Too many children were present to attempt disarming Victoria. She stayed just beyond reach, circling the group until she finally stopped and made eye contact with Ben.

She's crazy.

When the cold blue eyes aligned with hers, Ben knew she was in trouble. There was nothing in them, just a sort of manic dullness that didn't make sense.

"God, you got fat!" Victoria laughed hysterically. "I know, I know, pregnant. That's why Don didn't want you to get knocked up. He knew you'd never recover and would be a fatass the rest of your life like all these bitches around here. God, women, buy a Stairmaster!"

"What do you want, Victoria?" Ben swallowed hard, her mouth so dry the words didn't form easily.

Mark was too far away to reach her, which was for the best. Kira, along with the other kids from the race, was pushed behind a line of mothers. Ben had to believe her family would be okay, no matter what Victoria did to her.

"Well, you, of course." Victoria held the gun in her hand, the narrow, but deadly barrel aimed at Ben's chest. Only the race course separated them, thirty feet at most. "You couldn't just get raped and traumatized, could you? No, you had to survive, and then you've got the nerve to get married. Oh no, Bennie, that's not for selfish sluts like you. I wanted Don, but he wanted you. I don't want this Mark. He's a farmer, and that is disgusting, but I know you love him."

"No," Ben gasped when Victoria turned the gun on Mark. "Please, please don't hurt him."

The gun swung back as Victoria's insane giggle erupted once more. "Oh, I do like to hear you beg. I'd already decided to kill you anyway, Bennie. I like the pain to keep growing. With you dead, the farmer and his brats will be destroyed and ya know, I really like that."

"No!" Mark shouted, and when Ben looked she saw he was running toward them. Victoria turned her face to him but kept the gun aimed at Ben's chest. Her crazy gaze met with Ben's again, and as if in slow motion, she smiled, pulling the trigger without hesitation.

The shot seemed to reverberate in stereo, all over, but not at the same time. More important than the sound, Ben was slammed to the ground. She'd never been shot, and realized a moment later she hadn't been.

Thomas lay over her as Victoria screamed. During the shot, Mark and the surrounding men had tackled her and were scrambling for the gun. The woman was screaming profanities, and from the men's curses, probably biting and kicking as well. Ben didn't notice any of that, though, because Thomas wasn't moving.

"Thomas, Thomas?" She pressed against his lanky body, the lifelessness she found there overriding any discomfort from the race stake poking her back.

"He was hit, Ben," Rachel Spears, Kira's teacher said calmly. "Tina! SaraJean, call the ambulance! Here we go, let's turn him and get pressure on the wound."

"Okay, okay." Panic threatened but was pushed aside in the face of helping Thomas, the boy who wanted to call her 'mom'. "Thomas, you are in so much trouble."

Ben kept talking to him as she and Rachel, directed by two of the local nurses who were also mothers, maintained pressure on the wound high on his chest. The blood that had poured at first seemed to ease back to a sluggish pace. Mark held a fighting Kira as she tried to get to Thomas.

The ambulance finally arrived, Dr. Harper and his partner on board for the ride to the helicopter pad. Covered in blood, Ben shuffled back when Dr. Harper gently put a hand to her shoulder. They assessed Thomas's condition, gave reassurances, and were gone in minutes.

"Ben, honey, we have to go." Mark shook her shoulder gently when she just stared at the blood on the ground, so grotesquely black on the bright, happy, innocent grass.

The police had arrived while she'd been helping Thomas, and the screaming had stopped she noticed. There was talking but it was the quiet, shocked kind that didn't allow for actual words to be heard, just the murmurs.

"Ben, Mom?" Kira cried. "Thomas said you'd be our mom. He's okay, right? Right, Mom? He's okay?"

The little girl's sobs broke the rest of Ben's daze, and once again demanded she be the anchor. One of the moms handed her a button-down, flannel shirt probably from the backseat of someone's car. Ben held her arms so the bloody places were covered and pulled Kira close as Mark led them both to his car.

"I'm going to kill her!" Victoria screamed.

Mark jerked around, putting himself between the yelling woman and Ben and Kira.

Two Kansas City officers fell, and somehow Victoria grabbed a gun. That was as far as she got. Teddy was there. Within striking distance, he reached out and punched her in the face, knocking her out cold with a single strike.

Ben watched as he wrenched the gun away and threw her into the waiting police car. He put on handcuffs, pulled out zip ties, and locked her feet together before closing the door. The two officers were pale and shamefaced, but quiet, unassuming, sweet Teddy just cuffed both of their shoulders in camaraderie, nodded to the crowd, and got into his car.

"Okay, honey, let's go see your brother." Ben readjusted her weight. Kira was nearly too heavy for her to carry, but she didn't feel it. "We've got to go check on him, and after that we'll get him dinner. I know he'll be hungry, and I can never remember all the garbage he requires."

"It's not hard, Mom." Kira laughed through her tears, sniffing and rubbing her nose into the borrowed shirt. "Three double cheeseburgers, two chicken sandwiches, extra lettuce and no mayo. Two large fries, three yogurt parfaits, two cherry pies, and if Dad's buying, a large chocolate shake."

"See, how am I supposed to remember all that?" Ben teased because it was a long ride to KC and they needed to keep their heads.

The drive Mark made in record time gave her too much time to think. The sky darkened as they drove north, and Ben thought she'd be sick. If she had run when she had the chance, Thomas would be all right.

* * * *

An excruciating hour passed before a doctor emerged into the waiting room. Mark didn't know how he kept it together through the drive and the wait. Patience. His mother had always praised that trait as a gift from God. Mark prayed for just one more gift in the life of his nephew.

"Mr. Dougstat? I'm Doctor Lindon. You're Thomas LeDoux's guardian?" a petite young woman in surgical scrubs asked.

"Yes, I'm his uncle. His aunt, his sister." Mark pointed to Ben who was still holding Kira on the waiting room's sofa. "How is he?"

"Well, he obviously had good on-site care and in transport." The doctor rubbed the back of her neck. "The bleeding was nearly stopped when they arrived, but he went into cardiac arrest. We've got him back, and Doctor Johnson is finishing up now. The bullet hit a difficult spot, very close to his jugular, on impact, and near the spinal cord on the exit. I repaired the veins, cauterized some, and we gave him a lot of blood, but we think... he's young and strong, Mr. Dougstat. It might take a little while for him to come out of anesthesia because of the blood loss, but I'm very hopeful he will make a full recovery with time."

"Oh, thank God." Mark fell to his knees in relief. "Thank God, thank God. Thank you, Doctor. Thank God."

"When may we see him?" Ben's question made him look and he realized she'd moved closer. Kira was still on her lap, but she was by his side. Always by his side. She tugged his shirt sleeve and Mark leaned into her, her touch a tender mercy he needed, if only for a moment.

"As I said, my associate is finishing the surgery. He'll go to recovery after. It'll be at least another hour while the nurses get him settled and the doctor sees him. I'll have a nurse get you immediately after they finish,"

Dr. Lindon promised. "I'll be available for questions when I make rounds in three hours, and if Thomas's doctors require me I'm on campus."

"Okay, thank you." Ben's reply was more than Mark could do, and for the millionth time he was grateful for her strength.

"Did you understand all of that, Kira?" he asked when they were alone in the room

"He died," Kira sobbed. "Cardiac arrest means his heart stopped."

"He didn't die, honey. Yes, his heart stopped." Mark chose his words carefully because lying to Kira was like outsmarting a super computer. "But doctors and surgeons can do amazing things. That's why there's CPR and defibulators, squirt. The doctors got his heart beating again. We'll see him in half an hour, and he'll wake up."

"Probably starving," Ben added, and he smiled at her, always trusting her to help him find balance. "No mayo on his chicken sandwiches, right?"

"Right." Kira's sobs were heavy and deep and wouldn't quit despite their reassurances. She'd been holding a lot of her worries inside, and he couldn't blame her for the breakdown. "I love him so much. He's my best friend, and I don't hate him even a little."

"I know, honey. He knows it too," Ben said, and Mark could see her stroking Kira's head as she did the same through his own hair. "We'll see him soon, and you can tell him. You too, Mark."

"Yeah." He forced himself to his feet and away from the drugging comfort of her touch. "Here, Ben, hand over the squirt. I don't want you to hurt yourself."

He needed his wife to have a break, but he also needed to hold one of his babies, especially while the other was so hurt.

Chapter 21

Ben passed Kira into Mark's waiting arms, the little girl latching eagerly onto him. Without her weight, Ben's muscles expanded again, the discomfort growing exponentially. She didn't care. Guilt ate at every part of her as she waited. So many different choices could have been made, and she'd made the wrong one at every turn, and Thomas had paid the price.

The half hour went surprisingly fast as they sat in mostly silence. Mark held tight to Kira, and Ben understood the need. It would be a long time before they were comfortable without the kids in their arms.

At nearly dinner time the hospital was busy with meal trays being carried to the less critical rooms. The scent of steamed peas and chicken filled the halls over the antiseptic and sick smells. Thomas was past the regular rooms, and in one encased with glass.

"Just a few minutes," the nurse said quietly as she led them into Thomas's room. "The breathing tube will be removed within the hour. He's coming out of anesthesia slowly, but his stats are good, improving almost every minute. Go ahead and talk with him. If you have questions, I'll do my best to answer, otherwise Doctor Lindon will be around soon for rounds."

There was a small chair beside the bed that looked much too big for the tall, skinny kid occupying it. His dark hair was a mess, sticking up all over, and the grotesque tube from his mouth was so foreign and wrong it hurt Ben to see it.

He'd stepped in front of a bullet for her.

"Thomas," Kira whispered, holding his limp hand to her cheek. "You big dummy. I'm gonna give you chesties and purple nerples for a week when you're out of here. Don't you know you're supposed to save the girl and not get shot? Only losers get shot."

The nurse snorted in laughter, but Ben wasn't surprised. Kira loved her brother, they all knew it, and that affection and adoration was shown most purely in teasing.

"He did it to impress Melody." Mark's words were a little forced, but he touched Thomas's dark hair reverently. "He'll be getting his booboos kissed for the next few months. She'll probably make him cookies twice a week too."

"Then he'll expect us to name the babies after him," Ben added, kissing his forehead tenderly. "Thomasina and Thomasia, right, big boy?"

They stood around his bed, each saying small things, loving things. Ben didn't want to leave his side, but the five minutes ticked by at breakneck speed. Leaving him when he was so hurt went against everything in her, and the way Mark held tight to his hand told her she wasn't the only one who was having trouble stepping away.

The nurse checked in again on minute six. "In a half an hour you can visit again, and hopefully we'll have the tube out."

"Thanks." Mark nodded to the nurse and then bent and kissed Thomas's sweat damp brow. "No pinching the nice nurses, young man. You've made me proud since the day you were born, and I know you're going to wake up so I can tell you how much I love you."

"I love you, Thomas." Kira clung to the side of his bed.

"He knows," Mark whispered as he carefully pulled her away and carried her out of the room, both of them looking over his shoulders as they went.

"Thomas." Ben kept her words quiet, just for him, as she pushed herself to her aching feet. "We'll be right outside. Take your time if you need it, honey, but wake up for us."

* * * *

Ben and Kira lay side by side on a hospital sofa asleep. It was after midnight, and they'd visited with Thomas three more times before succumbing to exhaustion. They'd gotten their hands squeezed, and that had reassured them both. Mark had encouraged them to sleep. He wasn't sure if he would be able to until Thomas was okay.

During his last visit, alone, Thomas had opened his eyes. Fuzzy and confused, his brown eyes looked up at him with the trust of the child he'd once been, expecting him to make it all better. There wasn't a damn thing he could do about the wires, blood or pain though. He'd spent the time staring into his boy's eyes and praying.

Mark was so damn proud. He wanted to throttle Thomas for putting himself in danger, but he'd saved Ben and the babies, and he couldn't argue that. One crazy woman had nearly destroyed his entire family, but by God's grace they would heal and continue on.

He paced to the waiting room's window. It was a smaller, private room for families to gather for the long term. He pulled out his cellphone and checked the time. The call he needed to make couldn't be avoided any longer.

He would be able to get hold of Kimmy. A message earlier might have been appropriate, but he hadn't bothered. Kimmy rarely checked her messages, and even when she did she didn't return his calls. He dialed her work number and waited, resting his head against the cool glass of the hospital window overlooking the nearly empty visitors' parking lot.

"Doctor LeDoux," she greeted in French.

"Kimmy, it's me. We've had some issues here."

"Oh?" Her level of disinterest assured him she hadn't put aside whatever she'd been working on when the phone rang.

"Yes. Thomas was shot in the chest. There was a sociopath in town, she boiled over, and Thomas was shot saving my wife." He braced for her response, ready for the worst, because he deserved it.

"Will he live?"

No change in her tone, barely concern. He was the closest he'd been to taking a drink in ten years because he was eating his heart out. It galled him that the one person in the world who should have had a connection with Thomas, probably hadn't even looked away from her file.

"Yes. His breathing tube is out now, he squeezed my hand and has his eyes open," he explained. "Kimmy, it was a freak thing. He's got a long road to recovery, but the doctors say he will recover well."

"Good. I'm glad." The perfunctory, polite reply was all he could expect from her. Had he been thinking, he would have guessed her response right on. "I found the most fascinating strain of virus yesterday, Mark. You'd never believe how utterly simple yet complex a single strain organism can be."

He gritted his teeth against his anger at her rapid subject change. He didn't know why he expected her to change, but every time she proved how little she cared about her children, he wanted to scream. "Are you coming to see your son?"

"Why? He'll recover, and we both know who he wants and it's not me." Her honestly surprised tone irritated him even more than her words. "You do fine with him, Mark. I trust you. Pierre trusts you too."

"My wife is a teacher, so she's handling the paperwork." The sarcasm and bitterness in his tone was unavoidable.

Stephanie Beck

"One of our favorite aides is dyslexic. Pierre has refined his opinion of the disorder," Kimmy explained. "Speaking of Pierre, I only have another minute before we are set to begin. Is there anything else?"

"Why, Kimmy? Why the hell would you have kids just to give them away?" His usually guarded opinion burst out. He was tired and he was afraid, and it infuriated him the boy he loved like his own meant nothing to the ones who had birthed him.

"They're brilliant children, Mark. Pierre and I are scientists of a different quality, and not reproducing would have been an abomination." She paused and let out a long sigh. "I know I'm not the mother you would have me be. I won't apologize for it, because I'm content and so are they in this arrangement. And you can't tell me you aren't happy having them."

"I love them like they're my own, so I can't imagine why you can't."

"That's okay, Mark, you don't have to understand. You just have to get them safely to adulthood and hope for the best. Your wife is all right? She's pregnant, correct?"

"Yes, she's six months pregnant with twins. She had to have a few stitches, but like I said, your son saved her life."

"You might as well claim him as your own, Markie." Her reply showed a rare glimpse of the sister he remembered from his youth. "He doesn't call us 'mom and dad' anymore, which is for the best. If you're waiting for permission from me, you have it. You're his father in every way that matters. You are Kira's father as well, and have been since they were small. Keep me updated if he has issues or requires further medical care we may assist with."

"Okay, Kimmy, I'll do that."

Mark blew out a heavy breath as he closed his phone. He loved his sister, he really did, but his parents never should have sent her off to a special school when she was ten.

The parking lot started showing signs of a new day. It was still a precarious hour, but he supposed shifts changed. Puddles gathered the excess of the night's rain shower. At least the sun was shining and no more storms were forecasted.

Across the main road was a mini-mall with a flower shop and dollar store. There was also a liquor store. Mark still held his phone in his hand. He looked at it when it crunched a bit.

He'd broken the screen. It pulled him out of his thoughts. Liquor offered no solace for him. It only took the pain away temporarily, but could affect a situation forever. He wasn't doing it, damn it. Never again.

"Are you okay?"

He looked away from his broken phone. There was another reason he refused to succumb to the temptation that was slowly ebbing as he focused more calmly. His struggle must have shown because Ben eased away from Kira in an awkward shift.

He needed to get her home. She should be tucked into their bed, comfortable with the babies. Kira too, but neither female was leaving, and wouldn't until Thomas was out of the woods.

He was grateful they both were close. He should have known in the quiet his demons would make themselves known. Ben slid her arm around his waist and he pulled her close, feeling everything line up once more. He'd gone it alone for long enough to know temptation would have been controllable before buying anything, but it was better with Ben. Everything was.

"I'm okay." The hall was quiet, and his words barely disturbed that as he rubbed her back through her flannel, careful of her stitches. "I talked to my sister. I told her that her son had been shot saving my wife. I explained how we'd nearly lost him. She told me about her newest virus discovery."

"It's unfathomable, isn't it?" Ben asked quietly. "How anyone could set aside all the love those two kids are full of, for any reason, is beyond me. Mark, I feel sick when I think about what happened. If we'd stayed home--"

"Then something worse would have happened." He knew the way her mind worked, and she'd been blaming herself. The message he'd had from the sheriff on his phone put the whole situation in perspective. "The police found her car. Victoria had gas and other accelerants in her trunk, and when they asked her about them she said she'd checked by the farm first. She'd been watching us for days, even called yesterday. Her other plan had been to burn us."

"What?"

Maybe it hadn't been the right thing to share, Mark thought when she paled.

"Ben, I only told you so you'd know it was her, not you. None of this is your fault. It never has been from day one. She's crazy, and there's no foolproof defense against that. We did our best, I believe, and had all the help we could have had. We can't give up now." He held her close as the silence from her stretched. "Ben?"

"I... He's got to get better, Mark," she whispered. "I don't know what we'll do if he doesn't."

She was close to losing it and Mark couldn't let that happen. The pain, physically and emotionally, was more than she needed to handle with the babies as well. If she crumbled, she'd hate herself even more.

"Oh my gosh, is that a liquor store?" She pulled out of his arms, and he thanked God for showing her a focus. "Is that what you were thinking about out here? I'm such a selfish cow. Can I help?" She turned to him with earnest eyes, his practical Ben pulling the part of her that had been so close to breaking, back to center. "I know you have your group. Do you want me to call Pastor Reid for you?"

He pulled her close again. She understood everything about him and even if she didn't really get it all, she loved him anyway. It was the acceptance the kids showed him, and he'd found that quality of love with another human who he would spend the rest of his days making a life with.

"Thanks for the offer, but I'm okay now. It was close for a few minutes, but I'm okay. I promise."

"If you're sure…"

He nodded, and she looked like she might cry again.

"What's wrong?"

"Thomas asked if it was all right if they called me 'mom.'" There were tears in her eyes when she made the announcement. "Because of the babies, he said, so they don't get confused."

"Oh yeah?" Kimmy's words echoed in his mind. "Makes sense to me, if that's what they want. If it's okay with you?"

"Definitely." She pressed a kiss into his shoulder, the fabric doing little to detract from the affection and warmth he felt with the peck. "They want to call you 'dad' too."

"That--that would be okay with me." He held her closer and was quiet for a long minute. "God, is this finally over? Can we really just love our kids and work our jobs and be a family? I need some peace."

"Handsome, we've got twins due in a few months, a teenager on the cusp of some major life decisions, and a little girl who is going to be a teenager before we know it." Ben squeezed him and laughed. "I think 'peace' is a little much to ask for. But without Victoria hanging over our heads I think we'll be able to really enjoy the everyday sort of turmoil."

"I guess you're right." He chuckled quietly. "Maybe we'd better keep the security system in place in case Kira fulfills her angry promises to be a horrible teenager to get me back at me for not letting her eat candy for breakfast."

"It's probably a good thing we're in this together." Ben hugged him hard. "I was one of those horrible teenagers not too long ago. You've got experience with babies, and we've both had to make the decisions Thomas is coming up on. Between the two of us and our friends, I think we'll do fine."

"Together." Mark swallowed away the last of his disquiet with Ben in his arms, bolstering him once more against the challenges they had to face. "We can do it all together."

Chapter 22

Four months later, Halloween

"Eew, gross. Mom! Danny pooped on me."

With her hands full with Danny's little sister and the phone pressed to her ear, Ben bit back a laugh. Kira really didn't think it was funny when the breastfed babies let loose with projectile mustard poop.

"It's okay, honey, you've got time to change. Thomas, can you help your sister, please? Aunt Willy, I would love to talk but I need to get the kids moving."

"A houseful of children," Willy said, and Ben could nearly feel her shudder across the phone. "You're crazy, you know that, right, young lady? What were you thinking, marrying a farmer? You know how they reproduce. Mark my words, you'll be pregnant and barefoot for the next ten years."

"Nothing would make me happier than to have a large, healthy family with the man I love. I'm sorry, Aunt Willy, but I really need to go. Take care and I'll see you soon. We love you."

"Yes, well, I love you too. Take care of those babies, and I need more pictures. Mable got a whole set of the fancy ones from her granddaughter."

"Okay, I'll make sure I get some sent the first of the week."

Ben hit the off button on the cordless and tossed it aside, using her other hand to halt her wiggling daughter long enough to secure her diaper. Maureen was the champ of kicking out of her diaper.

"I don't do poop." Thomas's voice had deepened in only a few short months and never ceased to startle Ben. He was back to his normal self after having the summer to recover, and also avoided the messy diapers like the plague.

"Just bring Danny here for me," she called. "I'm almost done with Maureen, and I've already got the stuff."

Taller, skinnier, and smellier--though Ben did her best to keep the young man in body wash, deodorant and cologne--Thomas brought in his tiny namesake, Daniel Thomas. The little boy, not quite eight pounds at two months old, cooed happily at the big boy who cooed right back. They were good together, both of the older kids were amazing with the twins they considered their siblings.

"Here you go, Mom." Thomas handed her the baby wrapped only in a fresh blanket. "Oh, and he crapped all over your bed, a little Halloween treat for you."

"Take your sister." She handed him Maureen after she'd set Danny down on the blanketed floor. "Can you put a bib on her, please? I'd like to be able to get to the party without having to change her again."

"Can do." Thomas cuddled the green clad little girl complete with a tiny bow in her fine black hair. "Come on, cutie pie, or should I say sweetie pea?"

Ben cooed to her son, her first born, who'd decided he needed to be out a month early. Maureen was a follower so far, and had happily joined her brother within minutes. They'd been healthy, good stock her aunt had said during her brief visit.

The babies had stayed a week in the hospital, but once home, they'd thrived. Ben hadn't slept a full night in weeks, but she didn't care. Mark didn't care about his interrupted nights, and even though they complained at times, Kira and Thomas didn't mind so much either.

The last Halloween had been spent recovering after a nightmare. Parts of it were more recent. Only a month before Steven's body had been found in an Arkansas river, and the Victoria situation had reared its ugly head for a moment.

The ugliness was done and this year for Halloween, Ben had her peas in a pod. Her straw hat was hanging next to Mark's baseball cap, and they were all ready for the local Halloween parties.

"There you go, little man." Ben tucked her short legged boy into his green suit and zipped it. "You are so handsome. You'll have to coo extra sweet for big sis, now that you smell nice. You traumatize the poor girl every time you let loose when she's trying to help."

"It's okay, Mom." Fresh from her shower, Kira was dressed in all purple with a round tag around her middle declaring her the sharpest crayon in the box. "I know he can't help it. I'll shove his face in the watering trough when he's a lot bigger, though, don't worry."

"Oh, I believe it." Ben smiled. "You look good."

"Yeah, CeCe and Tory are gonna flip when they read this," Kira said mischievously. "The ones they have just say 'green' and 'blue.'"

"It is a cute idea." Mark had thought of it the night before and she'd helped Kira run with it. "Are you ready for trick-or-treating?"

"Yeah, Thomas is only wearing his helmet this year, and is only going to take me to three blocks."

"He's seventeen, honey," Ben reminded her. "And we've got three parties full of games and candy."

"I know. It sucks that he's old."

"He sure is." The transition into young adulthood for Thomas was nearly as hard on Kira as it was on him. They were dealing well, even if the pouting happened often. Ben stood and lifted Danny in her arms, laying a kiss on his bald head. "Is your dad in yet?"

"I'm in, I'm in." Mark hurried through the living room door and into the bedroom. "Ah, hell."

"Danny pooped on the blanket!" Kira announced unnecessarily.

"And you just couldn't have taken it to the laundry room." Ben winced when she heard Mark curse.

"Right, it was gross, and I was full of poop," Kira whispered, horrified.

"Okay. Can you help Thomas watch the minions while I help Mark get ready?"

"Yep." Kira plopped down on the floor. She wasn't allowed to hold the babies while walking, so she sat on her butt next to Maureen and held her arms appropriately. "Load him up. No pooping, mister."

Ben placed her little boy in Kira's arms and tossed the baby paraphernalia in the laundry basket beside the TV. It was the catchall for pacifiers, blankies, rattles, clean diapers, wipes, butt cream and socks. The twins were always kicking off their socks.

She entered her bedroom, also full of baby stuff. The bassinet the twins shared was near her side of the bed, along with a dresser full of baby clothes beside Mark's.

There was talk of an addition in the spring, and Ben couldn't wait.

"I'm almost ready," Mark called, the shower turning off and a curse coming from behind the only partially closed door.

"Take your time, handsome." She nudged the bathroom door open and watched him dry off his big, furry body. "Kira's going trick-or-treating with Thomas as soon as I give them the okay. Then we'll meet them in an hour at Mercer's party with Danny and Maureen."

"We've got an hour?" He immediately perked up with the announcement. He looked up from his drying, and his eyes darkened as her words took effect.

"Yep, and the babies are happy. They just had their baths, and were nursed. Hopefully they'll nap in their swings when I turn them to vibrate," she added. "What in the world could we do for an hour while the kids are gone? Any thoughts? Maybe we could whittle or wash windows or something."

Naked and only half dry, Mark headed for the bedroom. He stripped the soiled blanket off the bed, tossed it in the bathroom, and stretched out on the sheeted bed.

"Ah, gotcha. I could use a nap too," Ben admitted, and on her way past him got her butt spanked. "All right, all right." She laughed at his growl. "Five minutes."

"I'm starting without you."

"You would." She rolled her eyes and left the room, careful not to open the door too far as both kids were sitting at the table with their treat bags.

Thomas, the astute little angel, already had both babies in their swings with music and vibrations. "Well, are you ready for trick-or-treating?"

"Yes, finally." Kira hopped up and down with her pillowcase at the ready. "Come on, Thomas! We gotta stop by the Carmichael's house. They always give out full-sized candy bars. Bye, Mom. See you at the party."

"One hour," Ben said firmly, though Kira's excitement was pretty much matched by her own. "Wait to eat the candy until we can check it unless it comes from someone we know."

"We only go to people we know, Mom." Thomas grabbed his own bag, the biggest pillowcase they had in the house. "You sure you only need an hour? I can go a couple more blocks."

"You are way too smart." Ben laughed, Kira already out the door. "Would an hour and a half kill you?"

"Nope." Thomas shrugged. "Especially if I got another half an hour for curfew next Friday."

"Movies in KC?" Ben asked, the usual reason Thomas asked for an extension.

"Yep, Melody wants to see some stupid thing that's only playing there," he replied, scowling, but the girl had a pretty strong hold on his heart.

"Done, I'll even toss in twenty bucks to take her out for dinner," Ben added, and cuffed his shoulder when his grin turned wolfish, so much like his uncle. "Scoot. Be good."

"Always," he replied. "Have fun."

She followed Thomas through the laundry room, starting the waiting load so she could do the blanket later. She checked outside to see Kira dancing around Thomas's truck. "Have fun, Kira. I love you both!"

"Love you too, Mom!" Kira shouted, climbing into the truck. "Come on, Thomas, tell her you love her or she'll worry."

"Love you, Mom," Thomas yelled over his shoulder with a little wave because Kira was partially right. Ben would worry regardless of the declaration, but it was right to always leave each other with the words.

Ben turned on the security system, a long habit they all continued though the threat was currently locked in a maximum security prison in Illinois. Victoria was destined never to see civilian life again after receiving life after life sentences for more murders than Ben could think about.

She checked on the babies, safely buckled into their seats and already snoozing. After looking them over a second time, she turned on the baby monitor and headed to the bedroom.

They'd only made love twice since the delivery. She'd hoped for more, but her cesarean wound still ached at times. Six weeks in theory had seemed like forever before the surgery, but she'd learned the doctors weren't kidding with the wait advice. Even after those weeks had passed, fatigue, the added weight, breastfeeding, exhaustion and stretch marks had all made the first time a worry for her.

She smiled as she left the door open a crack, the babies just in sight. Some physical things may have changed, but the important things had remained.

No awards would have been given out, but the intimacy had helped renew the promises between them. Mark made her feel desirable, sexy and beautiful even when she had bags under her eyes and more extra skin than she knew what to do with. In return she'd given him all her attention and done her best to make sure he knew he was all man and all hers.

Ben entered the evening-dim bedroom. It was a cluttered mess. But with the blanket out and the window open it smelled like only babies and Mark again, her favorite things.

He'd lit the room's single rose-scented candle on the bedside table and was warming a small bottle of lubricating oil between his palms. He'd started without her all right, taking the waiting time to do the things that were sure to make her relax so they could enjoy each other.

He hadn't noticed her yet, and turned the bottle in his hands. She watched him frown down at the words on the label. It was a new addition to their bedroom life since the breastfeeding changed things. It was important to him to make sure he never hurt her, and the knowledge that he would cut off his arm before hurting her, made her eyes sting.

He looked up and frowned more. "You okay, honey?"

She nodded, too choked up to talk. She didn't want to cry, was just a little overwhelmed by the sudden love welling in her soul.

"Sure?" he asked, his lopsided smile hesitant.

She nodded again, stepped over the case of baby wipes in the middle of the floor, and cuddled up beside him on the bed. She hugged him hard and kissed his bare shoulder. "I just love you."

"I love you too." His confusion turned into warmth. She basked in it, because he only shared that warmth with her. He was a good guy for everyone, but the best parts were all hers. "Are we still using this hour for making love, or do you need a nap?"

"We have an hour and a half, and we are definitely using it to make love." She reinforced her words by running her fingers up his abdomen. "We've got time for naps when we're both in rocking chairs."

"I'll still want to be in bed with you." Mark set the lube bottle down beside his pillow and laid half over her, still careful of her stomach. He brushed a kiss across her neck. "Your freckles will need intense cataloging, and it's a job I'll always take seriously. Outside of bed I'll be the old guy who's always pinching his wife's butt in the grocery store and eyeing her cleavage in church when she bends over the dessert tray."

"I'll be the little old lady who loves you," she replied. "And puts up with your butt grabbing ways and wears v-necks to bake sales."

He kissed her mouth, lightly, teasingly, and began unbuttoning her shirt. "I'll steal your shawl," he promised, kissing down to her chin and neck. "And wash your dentures."

"I'll help you with your bunion cushions." She wiggled out of her shirt and gasped when he gently took her nipple in his mouth. "And tell you bald is sexy."

He was careful, so careful, with her breasts that were serving dual purpose for the next few months. She didn't worry about what he thought about her body, because she already knew. He loved her, the rest was just details.

"I'm going to love you so well, by the time we are old enough for our rocking chairs and great-grandbabies, you'll be ready for whatever comes next right beside me." Mark paused to look up her body to her face. "There wouldn't be a heaven without you, Ben, not for me."

She stroked his cheek, so dear; he was the means of everything wonderful in her life.

"I know exactly what you mean. You're my heaven right here on earth."

Meet the Author

Stephanie Beck loves romance. Whether it takes on everyday situations made harrowing by extenuating circumstances like Teaching Ms. Riggs or more erotic themes like Poppy's Passions, romance and love wiggle their way into most of what Stephanie writes.

It's hard to say what most women really think and feel, because every woman is and should be different, but Steph tries to find a balance of what an 'ordinary' woman can relate to and what they really want. With multiple worlds full of naughty-good fun running amuck in her brain, much more is to come from Stephanie Beck.

Stephanie's Website:
www.stephaniebeck.net
Reader eMail:
stephaniebeckauthor@gmail.com

Turn the page for a special excerpt of Stephanie Beck's

Unraveling Midnight

An entanglement with a werewolf brings unexpected turns.

Scott, a lone werewolf expelled from his pack, bends over backward
to give his kids everything he can—including knitting lessons for
his daughter. Learning to knit becomes much more appealing with
Lucy Jamieson as the teacher. His heightened senses tell him the
compassionate and beautiful human might be what he and his little
band need, yet getting involved with Lucy means exposing her to his
paranormal reality.

Although Lucy's childhood skewed her expectations of family, she
recognizes and respects Scott's desire to protect and provide for his kids.
When Scott is hit by a truck, Lucy offers to help with the kids--and gets
more than she bargained for after learning Scott's true nature...

On sale now!

Chapter 1

Scott's boys were going to be the death of him. He looked at the two young males rolling around the grass in a tangle of arms and legs. At least they were outside this time. He'd thought dealing with twins when they were infants was difficult. It turned out he'd only gotten a taste of hell in those years of bottles and diapers.

"All right, boys, get up. I want you running down to the trees and back a dozen times."

They groaned, but got to their feet. Ross and Greg were twelve and so near to puberty they reeked of the horrid promise. Mood swings, temper flares, and the almighty shifting time approached at a breakneck speed without apology. Their scents pledged within the next two years there were going to be major changes in his household dynamics. Scott wasn't ready.

"I bet I can run it twenty times," Greg said, kicking his shoes off.

"I can run it twenty-five," Ross challenged.

"Then do it," Scott ordered and watched them take off.

He blew out a sigh of relief. Maybe the monsters would get to sleep at a decent hour. If he wore them out, they were good little pups after dinner. If they were full of energy, things in the house started to get broken from all the roughhousing.

But that's the way things were when there were two adolescent werewolves under one roof. He now understood why his mother had gotten rid of all the furniture in the basement and had given him and his brothers mattresses. Even those had gotten torn up on occasion during wolf play or even screwing around as humans. Things had to be different in his house though, because it wasn't only him and the boys.

Scott turned and found the sweetness in his life. Jessie. Completely innocent and only six years old, she didn't deserve to live in an older-brother-proofed house. Scott did his best to wear them all out so she could have at least a little peace at home.

He frowned when he realized she was sitting on a bench with an adult. Usually his daughter was very reserved with other people, so he didn't worry about her talking to strangers. Being a werewolf led to a certain amount of caution in the young ones. They were taught early to hide their secret from strangers and to also be wary of outsiders. Scott found the scent of the adult. A female human, nonthreatening, but then no one seemed threatening until they did something horrible.

Like his former mate. Just the thought of what Tiffany had done to the kids put Scott's feet in motion. No one was going to get a chance to hurt his little girl and even if the human was innocent, it was up to him to decide, not Jessie.

* * * *

"What are you doing?"

Lucy turned and smiled when she found a pretty little girl had snuck up on her. She was dirty, her pigtails were crooked and she was missing three teeth. She looked exactly how a happy, healthy child in the summer should.

"I'm knitting," Lucy replied. "What are you doing?"

The child scratched at a scab on her elbow. "Playing. My daddy is running the boys and I was building a sand castle, but the sand in the sandbox isn't wet enough and I didn't bring my water bottle."

"Oh." Lucy pulled out a bottle of water from her lunch bag. "Here you go, honey. You can use this if you'd like."

"My name isn't honey," she said, accepting the water bottle. "I'm Jessie."

"It's nice to meet you, Jessie. I'm Lucy."

Jessie wrinkled her nose. "That's a grandma name."

She laughed. "Oh? Says who?"

"My daddy. My mom wanted to name me Lucy but Dad says that's an old fuddy duddy name like Martha."

Lucy laughed again. "Well, I guess it does have a certain old-school flare to it. Jessie does too. I had a grandma named Jessie."

"Really? I had a grandma Sophie but she died and my other grandma June kicked us out 'cause she thinks we're all evil." Immediately the little girl locked her lips shut and blushed. "I'm not supposed to talk about that."

Lucy smiled. "Don't worry about it, Jessie. I've already forgotten."

She'd gotten the chance to have her niece and nephew for a month while her sister concentrated on school, so she'd learned all about oversharing information and dealing with it. There was no use in making the child feel self-conscious. Sometimes they needed to say things and move on.

"Okay. What are you making?" Jessie asked, back to smiling.

"Today it's socks." She reached in her knitting tote. "Here is the first one and I'm half done with the second."

"No way." Jessie's eyes widened as she looked at the sock. "You actually made this with just string?"

"Well, yarn and four needles."

"Jessie."

The sharp tone made Lucy wince, but Jessie didn't seem to notice she'd done something wrong.

"Hi, Daddy. This is Lucy. She made a sock!"

Jessie's daddy didn't look too happy and Lucy tried to put on a friendly face. However besides unhappy, he also looked threatening. Deep scars on his cheeks spoke of past violence and his shortly buzzed hair didn't provide any relief from the harshness of his features. Every part of him said he was not only willing, but happy, to kick ass if needed. If Jessie hadn't called him 'daddy', Lucy wasn't sure if she'd have been able to get past his huge size to even offer a smile.

"Are you supposed to bother strangers, Jessie?" her father asked.

"She's not a stranger. She's Lucy and she makes stuff. Can you teach me to make this, Daddy?"

Lucy bit back a smile when the big, threatening man simply pinched the bridge of his nose. She couldn't hear him, but his lips moved as if he were counting to ten. Scary or not, this man was doing his best to live up to the 'daddy' title and, to Lucy, that made him more approachable.

"We've been visiting." Lucy offered her hand, hoping to cross the stranger-and-acquaintance gap. "I'm Lucy Jamieson. I own the yarn shop across the park over there."

He tentatively accepted her hand, eyeing it first like it was unexpected and maybe it was. For sure she'd bet his size and threatening features made for few random introductions. She'd also noticed over the month with the kids that adults at parks didn't interact much. They weren't out to make friends like the kids were. Lucy didn't see why they couldn't at least be friendly.

"Scott Terwolf. Thanks for entertaining her but, Jessie, you need to go play while we're here."

"Oh." The smile on Jessie's face fell and, though Lucy knew her dad wasn't intentionally being abrupt or mean, he'd popped her friendly balloon. "Okay. Thanks for talking to me, Lucy."

"You're welcome, honey. Have fun with your sandcastle. Don't forget the bottle."

Jessie's shy smile was a comfort after the abrupt change in plans, and when she grabbed the water bottle before running to the sandbox, Lucy knew the little one wasn't too upset. Beside her, Scott remained. She didn't have to look up because his large shadow made him known.

"The bottle was a fresh one, unopened, if you're worried," Lucy said, tucking the green sock Jessie had left on the bench back in her bag. "Not that I think she's going to drink it. I believe it's going to be more of a glue for the sand."

She looked out at Jessie instead of turning to Scott, expecting him to walk away like so many other parents did. They might visit for a moment, but during the spring when they'd found out she was aunt to kids who were leaving soon, making a connection didn't make sense for them. And now she was some childless lady sitting in the park with her knitting. Oh well, it was a beautiful day. She'd wanted to be outside for a while and she adored listening to the happy kids.

"I'm sorry for being rude."

She turned and found Scott sitting on the far side of the bench. But not too far. He wasn't a small man and took a good portion of the space, yet managed not to be too invading.

"You weren't rude," Lucy said and added a smile. "Just a daddy watching out for his daughter and I do understand the stranger issue needs to be reinforced often, especially at Jessie's age. Are those your sons over there?"

He turned and a grin came to his face. She'd been watching the boys play and roughhouse.

"Yep. I'm hoping if they get some energy out we might actually be able to watch a movie or something quiet tonight."

He sounded exhausted and Lucy laughed. "That sounds like a nice way to spend the evening. Though, well, good luck."

She winced when one of the boys tripped the other and they started tussling again. Scott's head whipped around and he let out a long, low whistle. The boys immediately perked up and got back to running.

"Great trick," she said, impressed. "They must have fantastic hearing."

His speed when he turned was a little disconcerting. "Yes, they do. It's a family thing. So you own the knitting shop? Do you have classes or anything?"

Surprised by the quick change in subject, Lucy paused a moment to collect her thoughts. "Ah, yes. I host weekly beginner classes as well as more advanced ones." She grinned, remembering Jessie's request. "Should I keep an eye out for you in the next few weeks?"

He laughed a little, but she knew when men thought knitting was ridiculous, and Scott was a long way from scoffing. "Actually, it's not very often Jessie finds something to light up about. We end up doing a lot of boy stuff and sports, so if she wants to try this, I wouldn't mind picking up the sticks."

"Needles," she corrected, more automatic than anything, but really she was charmed by his confession and willingness to make his daughter smile. "You know what? If you two come for class, I'll teach you all the important terms. We probably won't start with socks, but I think we could have you two knitting scarves by Christmastime."

"Lucy? Is that you sitting over there?"

Lucy shot Scott an apologetic smile before turning to the new voice. "Hi, Mrs. Kimmes. You look nice today."

The older woman always looked interesting. Lucy hoped she could pull off 'interesting' when she was older. Mrs. Kimmes wore a green skirt, purple knit top and bright pink lipstick. It all did kind of go all together with the mop of white curls on her head. A regular at the shop, the kind woman had gone out of her way to make Lucy's day often since she'd learned Lucy had lost her grandmother.

"Thank you, dear." Mrs. Kimmes stopped her powder pink scooter beside the bench. "And who is this handsome fellow sitting beside you like a giant lump of yummy?"

Ah, to be so free with words. Luckily, Lucy had known the older woman for three years and Mrs. Kimmes's mouth no longer surprised her. "This is Scott. We were discussing knitting lessons for him and his daughter."

"Both of them, huh?" The older woman's drawn-on eyebrows rose high. "Well, that's a newfangled thing. You don't look like one of those glittery men knitters, so I suppose you're just being nice. I like that. You won't find a better teacher than Lucy here. She's a good one. Why, she even took on an old hooker like me and made a full conversion."

Lucy was proud Scott didn't even wince at the old girl's announcement. He was a good sport and she supposed with all the kids, off the wall announcements weren't new.

"Oh, well I need to go. I'm meeting Wanda Fisher for lunch. Take care, Lucy, and you, young man, I know we've just met, but if you've got a mind to make eyes at this fine young woman, I suggest you not forget the roses. Too many young men these days go straight for the—"

"Mrs. Kimmes!"

The older woman smirked. "Oh, she's a bit of a prude too, but a nicer woman you'll never meet. I'm off. You two behave."

And like she hadn't come from nowhere to embarrass the heck out of Lucy, Mrs. Kimmes scooted away. Left once more with Scott, Lucy wasn't sure if she hoped he would walk away or if she wanted to have a chance to explain at least some of what the crazy woman had said.

"Hookers, huh?"

"Yeah, I didn't think you'd miss that one," Lucy said and tried not to blush. "She meant she used to only crochet. It's a kind of yarn work done with a single hook—which leads to those who enjoy crocheting being referred to as—"

"Hookers." He grinned. "I bet the old girl likes that. And the other? If I do sign up for class, do I need to bring roses?"

She'd bet hundreds of women had thrown themselves at him over his smile alone. Jessie hadn't mentioned a mother and Scott didn't wear a ring, so she assumed he was single. She couldn't be sure though.

"Hmm, no roses necessary for the first class," she said, indulging in a slightly flirty tone and hoping he would come to class so she could learn more about him. If nothing else, he was interesting to talk with and his daughter was adorable. She'd bet they'd both be pleasant company.

"I don't suppose you've got a card or something?"

"I can do you one better," she said and dug around the pocket of her knitting tote. "Here's a flyer with the beginners classes listed and you can come whenever. I have all the supplies and the starter kit I put together is really inexpensive, so if it doesn't click for you two, you won't be out more than ten dollars and a little time."

He accepted the flyer, looked it over and tucked it in his pocket. "I'll call soon."

Across the field, the boys started fighting.

"Oh, uh oh—"

"I think it's time to head home. Thanks again for being kind to Jessie and I'll be in contact soon."

He was up and gone in a flash, his speed shocking, but then, he was a dad and his boys were fighting. Jessie perked up for a second and followed and Lucy wondered if he'd whistled again. The move seemed a bit Von Trapp but it obviously worked. Lucy checked her watch and sighed before tucking her yarn away. Lunch break was over and the yarn shop wasn't going to run itself, no matter how nice it was outside.

www.ingramcontent.com/pod-product-compliance
Lightning Source LLC
Chambersburg PA
CBHW050748250626
47155CB00005B/1980